Bott

Wayfair V

One

by A.A. Albright

This is a work of fiction. Names, characters, organisations, places, events and incidents are either products of the author's imagination, or are used fictitiously.

Mailing List: http://www.subscribepage.com/z4n0f4
Website: https://aaalbright.com

ISBN: 9781549881305

Chapters:

1. Unfit for Humans

When it comes down to it, most of us put our own interests first. So when I turned the corner onto my road, and I saw two things happening at once, I did what most of us would do: I veered towards the event that actually affected *me*.

I did *incline* my head towards the macabre scene across the road. I mean, come on. A body was being wheeled into an ambulance and a twenty-something-year-old girl was being shoved into a police car, screaming, 'I dunno why I done it!' over and over again. It would have been remiss of me *not* to look. But I barely knew the residents in that house, and I was still far more concerned with what was happening at my own place.

'Are you kidding?' I asked the council worker who stood at the front steps, blocking my way. I peered over his shoulder. Two of his co-workers were hammering a sign to my front door. I stared at it: *No Entry. This property has been deemed unfit for human habitation, and has been condemned. Cross this line at your own risk.*

'Nope, not kidding. You've got every kind of mould there is.'

'I've never seen any mould.'

'Sorry love.' The council worker gave me a very un-sorry shrug. 'But it is what it is. The council are putting you and all the other residents up in hotels until you find somewhere else.'

'Can I at least go in and get my stuff?'

He sighed. 'Of course you can't go in. The sign says *No Entry,* doesn't it? Can't you read?'

'Yes, I can read. But it doesn't change the fact that I have to go in there. I have an exam on Friday. I need to study. And I have an interview today, too. I can hardly go in this.' I held my hands out, indicating my poorly-fitting supermarket uniform.

He opened the door of the council van and peered inside. 'Adrian Percy's already been and gone. So that makes you either Wanda Wayfair or Stacey Byrne. Which is it?'

'Um, Wanda?' I had to phrase it as a question. In fact, I had the sinking feeling that I'd be phrasing everything as a question for the rest of the day.

He grunted, then pulled three large, black plastic bags out and set them at my feet.

I gaped at him. 'Seriously? You packed up my stuff. Meaning you went *through* my stuff. *My* stuff.'

He curled his lip. 'No need to thank me. Oh, and here.' He pulled a crumpled piece of paper from his pocket. 'Seeing as you're Wanda, then this one is for you.'

I took the piece of paper: *This voucher entitles the bearer to a one month stay at the Hilltop Hotel, Warren Lane (Off Grafton Street), Dublin 2.*

'But … there *is* no Warren Lane near Grafton Street,' I said perplexedly.

The council worker shrugged, said, 'Take it up with someone who cares, love,' and proceeded to board up the windows of my former home.

≈

There was no telephone number on the voucher. Of course there wasn't. I mean, a wonderful day like this one didn't need much to make it better. I glanced at my watch. It was half past twelve. If I cut through St Stephen's Green, then I could make it to Grafton Street in ten minutes or so. Assuming I got settled into the hotel (if I could find it first) within the next half hour, I could probably make my job interview on time. I heaved one bag over my shoulder and took the other two in my hands, and then I ran.

Since I moved to Dublin at seventeen, I'd walked up and down Grafton Street countless times. There were many little roads leading off the main thoroughfare, but I'd never noticed one called Warren Lane. Given how perfectly my day was turning out so far, I doubted I'd find it today. A frantic search on the internet (via my mobile phone) was no help at all. There was a place called Warrenmount in Dublin 8, but nothing in Dublin 2.

Huffing and puffing, readjusting my bags a hundred times, I decided to search Grafton Street anyway. Because what else could I do? I was about halfway along the street, feeling evermore dejected, when a flower-seller wheeled a cart out in front of me and knocked me to the ground.

'Perfect,' I muttered, as they kept going without so much as a sorry. 'And I see you've left a fine mess behind you, too.' I picked a daisy out from under my right foot and stood up. The flower-seller had left a long trail of daisies behind them, a trail that led right up to a side-street called Warren Lane.

For a good minute or so, I just stared. For another minute or two, I shook my head. Eventually I snapped back to action, and turned into Warren Lane. I saw the hotel straight away, on the right side of the street. It wasn't on a hill, but I wasn't about to quibble. It was an old stone building, with stunning mullioned windows looking out onto the street. Wishing I had a free hand to wipe the sweat off my forehead, I rushed through the doors.

The foyer was large and cool, a welcome break after the June heat on the street outside. The ceilings were high, enormous black chandeliers hanging down – the largest, most decorative of all was in the centre of the ceiling. The walls were panelled at the bottom, with old-fashioned stonework at the top. Antique paintings of men and women decorated the upper part of the walls. Most of the subjects seemed to be stroking cats. I resisted the urge to look at each and every painting (difficult, when some of the people were wearing ridiculously awesome clothing), and denied myself the even stronger urge to sit on one of the foyer's many squidgy chairs.

Instead, I rushed to the reception desk. I was just about to put my hand to the brass bell when a short, curvaceous blonde appeared. She was dressed in a fitted jacket, tight skirt and high heels. On the lapel of her jacket was a large, gaudy, gold brooch shaped like a cat.

'Ah.' She glanced at the voucher in my hand. 'You must be Wanda Wayfair.'

I nodded, then asked breathlessly, 'Is anyone else from my house here yet?'

'Oh no, dear. Why on earth would you think *they'd* be here?'

To be honest, everyone in my house stayed in their own rooms, only coming out to occasionally use the loo or argue about who stole a tin of beans. We weren't close. We were barely civil. But still. It'd be nice to have *someone* familiar to grunt at. 'Because … well have the council put them somewhere else?'

She shrugged. 'I have no idea. You're the only one I have booked. Now … there's a bit of a problem with that too, love.'

'Well, of course there is. Let me guess. There's been a flood. Or a gas leak. Or a meteor's crashed into the hotel and *only* destroyed the room I'm booked into.'

'Wouldn't that be funny?' She laughed. I didn't join her. 'No. No, it's just that Maureen O'Mara was due to vacate her room this evening, only now she's decided to stay on a few more days. Now, the room's yours, technically. But well, you know what Maureen's like.'

'No.' I shook my head. 'I don't.'

'Oh, come off it. Everyone knows Maureen. And, that being the case, I didn't think you'd mind sharing.' She waved across the room, pointing towards a cluster of armchairs by the fireplace. 'There she is now.'

I turned and looked across the foyer. A tiny, skinny, grey-haired woman was sitting in an armchair, looking very nearly like she was being swallowed by it. On her lap was an enormous, leather-bound book. She wore a long, fitted black dress and a pearl-grey shawl. She looked at me, then opened her almost-entirely toothless mouth into a wide grin. 'Hello Wanda!' she called. 'Won't it be fun, us girls together!'

I made a non-committal shrug and turned back to the receptionist. 'Listen, can we sort this out later? For now I just need to get changed *really* quickly, because I have an interview in–' I glanced at my watch. '–forty-five minutes. And it's all the way in Berrys' Bottlers.'

'Oh.' She gave me an impressed looking nod. 'Aren't they doing well for themselves, that lot? Well, good luck to you, Wanda. I'm sure you'll get the job. Now, your room is on the top floor – thirteen flights up – or you could pop into the ladies' room just next to reception and I could have the bellboy take your bags up for later.'

'Yes. Yes, the second thing you said.' I couldn't manage any more small-talk. I grabbed what I needed and ran to the ladies' room.

I changed my clothes quickly, and I was just smoothing down my brown hair and thinking that, actually, this wasn't the worst day in the world. But then I saw it. My earlier sense of doom was reconfirmed. It sat there on the edge of the vanity unit, grinning at me. It was the oldest rat I had ever seen. Its toothless mouth was formed into a wide grin, and one of its scrawny, sharp-nailed little paws was raised in my direction.

I picked up my handbag, pushed my way out of the room, and ran to the bus stop on Dame Street as fast as my legs would carry me.

≈

I got to the bus stop with five minutes to spare, but my rush had made me thirsty, so I dashed into a nearby newsagent to grab a drink. I scanned the shelves for the cheapest, and spied something new.

'Berry Good Go Juice. Never seen you before.' I read the label, saw that it was well within my price range (dirt cheap) and paid for the drink. I drained the bottle quickly – it really was berry good – and was just about to throw it in the bin next to the bus stop when a newspaper came flying at me, thrown by a passenger in a nearby van.

'Today's is a good one,' said a gravelly voice beside me as I peeled the newspaper off my face.

I turned around. Normally, I'm not very good with faces. People often describe me as having my head in the clouds or being away with the fairies when it comes to such things as noticing hair-colour, eye-colour and so on. But even with my wonderful attention to detail, there are some people I'll never forget.

'Maureen O'Mara?'

The tiny woman from the Hilltop Hotel stood a few feet away, grinning at me. She wrapped her grey shawl tighter around her shoulders and said, 'I do like their papers. Great laugh so they are. Might keep you entertained on the bus, love. Keep your mind off your interview.'

I was just about to ask her how on earth she'd gotten from Warren Lane to Dame Street so quickly, when the bus pulled up. Clutching the newspaper in my hand, I stood back to let her go on ahead of me.

'Oh no, love. I'm not getting on. Just came to wish you luck.'

I had so many questions for Maureen. Why wasn't she out of breath? Why was she dressed like a lady from a horror film? Why did she act like she knew me? But I'd spent a lifetime avoiding the oddities of the world, and I wasn't about to become entrenched in them now. So I merely said, 'Well, bye then,' and boarded the bus.

As I took my seat, I did my best not to glance out. But I'm weak-willed, apparently, because I didn't so much look as I did gawp. As the bus pulled away from the stop, Maureen O'Mara stood on the street, waving me off and grinning like a madwoman.

I put the Daily Dubliner on the seat beside me, and picked up my beeping phone. I had ten text messages. All from my mother and her cohorts. I read the first:

We're moving again.

Then the second:

We'll send you the address when we get there so you can come for your birthday.

Pretty sure the rest of the messages would be similar, I put my phone away and picked up the paper. The headline on the front page was a little more exciting than usual – y'know, if you consider murder and mayhem exciting.

In Dublin's Scare City

Yes, you read it right. It's time to be scared, folks. The recent spate of seemingly random attacks in our formerly fair city has escalated. After days of people randomly knifing and strangling strangers, this morning, things got fatal. Connor Cramer of Cramer's Candles was killed with one of his very own candleholders, inside his very own shop. When the gardaí arrived at the scene, the attacker was still present, grasping the bloodied candleholder and screaming, 'I dunno why I done it!'

Last night, another attack victim, Adeline Albright, who calls herself an academic, managed to narrowly escape a similar attack.

'I suppose I was just lucky,' Adeline told our reporters. 'Listen, can I go now? I have to get home and feed the dog.'

As I read through paragraph after paragraph of questionable journalism, I wondered: could the scene across the road from my house have been connected?

The bus pulled up to the next stop, and a gust of breeze came in as more passengers boarded, whooshing the newspaper open right onto the *Rooms to Let* page.

I considered things. A rat-infested hotel that was free, or a room in a houseshare I could barely afford?

I put thoughts of In Dublin's Scare City aside, and scanned the listings.

Six hundred and fifty a month. Must smoke.

Six hundred a month. Vegetarians not welcome.

Eight hundred and eighty a month. Must be alright with roommates who watch a lot of porn.

Seven hundred a month. Swingers preferred but not required.

Two hundred and forty a month–

My eyes rounded. 'Two Hundred and forty!' I looked around, wondering if anyone had noticed my outburst, but they were all glued to their smartphone screens, so I returned to reading. '"*Number Three Westerly Crescent, Luna Park. Two hundred and forty a month. If interested, call before six.*"'

I chewed at my fingernails. Today had been a very strange day, but a room in Dublin for two-forty a month was possibly the strangest thing of all. As much as I was looking forward to sharing a room with Maureen (ahem), I decided that I might as well at least check if the price in the listing was a mistake. I picked up my mobile, and rang.

'Hi, I'm just calling about the room to let,' I said as soon as the phone was answered. 'The one for two-forty in the Daily Dubliner?'

'Oh. Right.' The voice sounded deep, male, and distracted. 'Sorry, what did you say your name was?'

'I didn't. It's Wanda Wayfair.'

'Wayfair? Seriously? And you want to live *here*?'

'It's not *that* unusual a name, is it? And look, I wouldn't be calling if I didn't need a room, now would I?'

'Hmm. Suppose not. But two-forty really doesn't bother you?'

I stifled a scream. 'Listen, is the room for rent or not?'

'It's for rent. Are you *sure* though? I mean … two-forty is a bit steep for the likes of you.'

I continued to stifle that same scream. It wasn't easy. 'Can you text me directions?'

'Well … I suppose. If you need them. But delete the message straight afterwards. Oh, and you have to get here before six, Wanda, because I go out at six.'

I hesitated a moment. Berrys' Bottlers was at a close-by industrial estate. If my interview there didn't take too long, then I could probably make it to Luna Park by six. Assuming the buses were on time, and I ran in between stops very *very* fast. 'I … yes. Yes I can be there before six.'

'Brilliant. Room's yours, so.' The phone hung up. A few seconds later, a text came through with directions.

≈

Berrys' Bottlers didn't seem to be having its best day. But who was I to judge? If anything, I sympathised with them. If my mother were here she'd blame today's oddities on the phase of the moon. Actually, that wasn't true. If my mother were here, she'd probably find nothing odd about this day at all.

Garda cars were in the company car park when I arrived, and two gardaí were questioning a tall, attractive, fifty-something blonde woman at the front doors. I stood awkwardly for a moment, wondering what to do, when a man approached me from the side.

'Wanda Wayfair?' he whispered, glancing anxiously at the scene in the carpark. 'I'm William Berry. You're here for the interview?'

'Um, yes,' I replied, doing my best not to stare. *This* was who I'd been emailing with? He was younger than I expected. And taller. And buffer. 'But … I can see there's been some trouble, so if you want to rearrange ...'

'This way, this way. Never mind all that,' he whispered, grabbing my hand and ushering me towards a staircase at the side of the building. 'We had a break-in last night, but it's all sorted now.'

He pushed open the door into a large office and stood back so that I could enter before him. Feminist me was enraged. Other parts of me … not so much. As I made my way in past him, I did my best not to stop and sniff. It was probably my most difficult feat of the day so far. Even at a semi-acceptable distance, his cologne smelled like heaven.

The office he ushered me into looked almost as perfect as he did. Everything seemed to be brand new. The filing cabinets gleamed. His desk was spotless, and there wasn't so much as a speck of dust on his computer.

'Sit down, Wanda. Make yourself comfortable,' he said. Now that he was no longer whispering, his voice was deep, chocolatey and delicious. 'Can I get you anything? Tea? Coffee? Water?'

As I sank into the plush new office chair he'd indicated, I shook my head and said, 'I'm fine, thanks.'

'All right then.' He sat behind his desk, chin in hands and looking far-too intently at me. 'Let's begin.'

It wouldn't be fair to say that I didn't pay attention to him after that point. Unfortunately, I was paying attention to all of the wrong things. The sea-green shade of his eyes. The dirty-blond locks of hair that fell across his tanned forehead once in a while. The lines of his biceps, bulging through his crisp white shirt.

'So you're happy with all of the other stuff the job entails?'

I dragged my mind back to the conversation. What other stuff?

'Um … yes? Yes, it all sounds great, Mr Berry.'

He rolled his eyes and gave a throaty laugh. 'We hardly need to be so formal, do we Wanda? Mr Berry is my father. And quite a few of my uncles as well. Call me Will. In fact, call me anything except Bill.'

It took a moment for me to stop staring at him before his joke sunk in. 'Oh. Hah! Bill Berry. Bilberry. That's a good one,' I said, before laughing just hard enough to make a fool of myself.

For some reason, he wasn't doing what other guys did when I acted like a moron. He wasn't wrinkling his nose, or staring at me like I had ten heads. Instead, he was laughing along with me and smiling like I was the most delightful thing he'd seen that day. But I must have been imagining it, because the most delightful thing that Will Berry had seen that day was his own reflection. Obviously.

'Well, I can't tell you how pleased I am that you like the sound of the job,' he said after a while, flashing his super-white teeth at me. His cheeks dimpled when he smiled. Movie-star dimples. Dimples that I wanted to lick. Dimples that made me imagine cherub-cheeked children (hopefully with more of his DNA than mine). 'Now, I see your driving licence is up to date, and you have your final accountancy exam this Friday.' He grinned even wider. 'On your birthday, too. Ah, twenty-one. I remember it well.'

I bit my lip, wondering just *how* recently he remembered twenty-one. He was definitely younger than thirty. In fact, if I had to guess at his age, then I would say he was about … the perfect age for me?

'So you'll be with Mike doing the wages on Wednesday. Unfortunately he'll be retiring on Friday, so Wednesday's the only day he'll have to show you the ropes in that regard. But I'm a chartered accountant too, so I can help you out after that. Now, I've told you about the other stuff you'll be doing with my aunt Alice tomorrow and

Thursday. You'll have to drive her there if that's okay. She's stubbed her toe again.'

'Oh. Drive her? Drive Alice … to the place. Yes, that's not a problem. Only I don't have a car, you see. Will that be an issue?'

He waved a hand. 'Oh, I wouldn't expect you to use your own car. In the company van, of course. And you'll get to use it yourself too, if you take the job. Little perk. I swear we won't be ringing you at twelve for lifts home from the pub. Too often.'

I forced out a laugh. He was being just as delightful as ever, but I was beginning to think that *maybe* I should have done a little less staring and a little more listening. 'Right. Well … do you have many more to interview before you let me know?'

He flashed his grin again. 'Wanda, Wanda, Wanda … you need to have more confidence in yourself, you know. Even if I had a hundred more applicants, I'd be ringing them up and telling them not to bother now I've met you. Job's yours, Wanda. See you at nine sharp?'

'Oh. Yes. Wonderful. Well, shall I …'

'Go?' He grinned at me again and I did my very best not to swoon. 'Much as it pains me to see you leave, yes, Wanda. The interview is over. The job is yours. And I'm very much looking forward to seeing you tomorrow morning at nine.'

2. That Old Familiar Feeling

If today was teaching me anything, it was that even if you've lived almost four years in Dublin, there are always new places to discover. I'd never heard of Westerly Crescent or Luna Park, but it turned out it was in Dublin 7, close to the Phoenix Park.

The moment I turned onto Westerly Crescent, I suddenly knew *why* I didn't know this place. The houses were large. Posh, even. The friends I'd made so far in Dublin tended to live in the sorts of places I did – small, rough, and affordable. But the guy on the phone had pretty much confirmed that the price was correct. All I could think of was that it must've been a box room he was renting. Or maybe a broom cupboard.

The houses in Westerly Crescent were arranged in a crescent shape (surprise!), facing onto Luna Park. The park was large, lush and well-manicured and, oddly, no one was sitting about drinking from a can. The houses along the road were just as well-kept as the park. The garden of Number One was especially lovely. The grass was cut in stripes (how did people do that?) and there wasn't a weed in sight. It had a sign next to the wall, saying: '*To Let. Call Luna Letting for details.*' There was no phone number on the sign.

Inside Number Two, a woman in dark glasses was pulling down the blinds. It was a bit early, but each to their own. Further down the road I could see a group of young men and women lying about on sun-loungers while various remote-controlled gadgets cut their grass, clipped their hedges and washed their windows.

It was five minutes to six when I arrived at the front door of Number Three. I picked up a rather fancy looking wrought-iron door-knocker, and prepared to let it fall. Before I could, however, the door was yanked open from the inside.

'You must be Wanda,' said a guy who looked about my age. He had shaggy, light-brown hair (not long, just messy) and dark brown eyes. And gosh, he was tall. I had to strain my neck to look up at him. 'I'm Max. Come in, come in, no time to waste.'

He reached for my bag, pulled it into the hall, and had the door slammed shut behind me the second I went inside.

'Is this all you have? Not a lot to move in with, is it? Oh, wait … is it one of those bags where the inside's bigger than the outside?'

I kept my glower to a minimum. 'No need to be sarcastic. My stuff's at a hotel. I'll go and get it if we're happy enough to, y'know, live together.'

He grinned. His teeth were long, super-white and, I have to say, a bit on the caveman side. If cavemen had excellent dentists and whitening bleach, that is. 'What, in case I was a maniac?'

I decided not to answer that.

Still holding my bag, he marched up the stairs. Assuming he wanted me to follow him, I ran up behind. His legs were a lot longer than mine, and by the time we got to the top I think I was a little red in the face.

He pointed to a closed door. 'That's my cousin's room. She's had to go away suddenly, but you'll like her. If you ever get to meet her.' He pointed to another room. The door of this one lay open. There was a large, neatly made bed, wall-to-wall wardrobes and shelves filled with books, cassettes and records. Real, actual records. 'That's my room,' he said. 'And no, I'm not a hipster. The cassettes and records were my dad's. I have all his old movies, too, boxed up under my bed. I don't play them, ever. I'm clumsy, y'see. Afraid I'll wreck them.'

I said, 'Oh. Right.' I'm sensitive like that.

Finally, we came to a room at the front of the house. The door was open, revealing a large double bed with a huge TV on the wall facing it. The bed was already made up with grey and plum sheets, pillowcases and a duvet, and a pair of fluffy purple slippers sat on the floor alongside. There was a desk with a cup full of pens and a swivel chair, a comfy armchair by the window overlooking the park, and a wall lined with fitted wardrobes.

'You've only got a shower in your en suite,' he said. 'But you can use the main bath whenever you like. Obviously, I'll try my best to keep it clean.'

'En suite?' I peered through a door beside the bed into a very large bathroom beyond. No, there was no bath, but there was a shower large enough for an orgy. (Did I really just say that? Well, I didn't mean it the way you think. Clearly.) A heated rail was lined with fluffy, plum-coloured towels. A candle was lit on the vanity unit, sending delicious waves of lavender wafting into the air.

I eyed Max. 'I feel like we've been talking at cross purposes. Is this room vacant right now? I mean the slippers, the towels … the candles… the massive TV … you seemed like you wanted me to move in right away, but the room looks like it's already occupied.'

He cleared his throat. 'Ahem. Well. Yes. It's very definitely vacant. An … um … a very wet dog got in last night. A stray. And he slept on every single bed in the house. Hence the fresh sheets and candles to make it smell a little bit better. And the slippers are just because … y'know … everyone likes a comfy pair of slippers.'

Okaaay. That made sense – in no way, whatsoever. 'But what's with the cup full of pens? Were they the last tenant's?'

He looked at the pens. 'No. I just like stationery. There're A-4 pads in the drawers, too. And some folders and paperclips and things. I mean, you can never have too much, can you?'

'Stationery?'

He nodded. 'Exactly. And I swear no one else has rented the place for weeks. I mean … it's not the sort of place many want to live, is it? That's why I rushed out and bought you some new slippers. I mean, I was going to get you a few more welcoming presents but … that'd just be weird.'

I didn't know how to respond to *any* of that. This was by far the nicest house, and the nicest neighbourhood, that I'd seen in quite a while. The guy's attitude was strange, to say the least. Even *without* the stationery fetish and the brand new slippers. But it was either this or a rat-infested hotel with a weird old lady.

I sat on the bed. 'Well, much as I'd like to find some reason not to stay … the room is perfect. The street is perfect. The rent is cheap as chips. And purple is my favourite shade for slippers. So I'm in, Max.'

He gave me a brief look of shock, then something more akin to panic crossed his features. He looked at his wristwatch, and the panic intensified. 'Good. Brilliant. Well, I have to go now. And I'll be out for the whole night.' He dashed out the door and to the staircase. 'Make yourself comfy, etcetera,' he called back to me as he sped away. 'There's milk – almond, soy *and* rice, seeing as I didn't know which you drank – and bread and stuff in the kitchen. Plenty more pens in the drawers in my room if you run out. What's mine is yours.'

'Wait!' I ran after him, leaning over the railing and staring down at him, but no sooner had I got there than he was already out the front door and slamming it shut behind him. 'I was *going* to ask you for a set of keys.'

≈

Considering I was in a strange room, I felt surprisingly at ease. Candles normally reminded me far too much of my childhood, but the lavender was calming. The second Max left I did what any sensible girl would. I checked the house for cameras or any other sign of weirdness. Then, deciding it was all on the up and up, I turned on the shower.

For the first time in years I found myself in a shower that actually worked. No fiddling with the dial only to wind up scalding or freezing. This water was perfect. And the fluffy warm towels and slippers afterward were even better.

I climbed into bed and turned on the TV, but I was only five minutes into my favourite vampire show when my eyelids began to droop. I set the alarm on my phone for five, making sure I had plenty of time to collect my bags from the Hilltop Hotel before work, and then fell into a fast and deep sleep. No dreams. Just the most perfect night's sleep I'd had for as long as I could remember.

I woke up feeling happy and rested, and showered yet again. Because … well, it would have been a waste not to.

At ten past five I stood by the window, running a brush through my hair and looking out onto the park. Hearing faint birdsong, I pushed the window open and leaned out, taking in breaths of fresh morning air. This place was far too lovely for the likes of me. With my luck, Max would turn up later on with an axe or a chainsaw, and that would be the end of that.

Just as I was about to close the window, I saw one very obvious reason why this was, indeed, too good to be true. A few houses away, at the corner of the estate, stood Number One, Westerly Crescent. The *To Let* sign had been removed. And the front garden that had been so perfectly manicured only yesterday … this morning, it was filled with weeds.

Stifling a scream, I forced myself to ignore the obvious, at least for now. I had a new job to begin. I could go over there and say my piece later on. Y'know, before I packed my bags and moved back to the rat-infested hotel. I mumbled a few things that I swear were sweeter and more innocent than they sounded, pulled on my suit, and went to the kitchen.

There was everything I needed to make a nice breakfast, but for now all I wanted was a cup of tea. With the kettle on, I looked through the fridge, wondering which of Max's many milks would taste best with tea. I erred on the side of caution and picked up the soymilk. Just as I was about to bring the carton to the counter, I heard a panting noise behind me. I turned and screamed, spilling the milk to the floor.

'Waste not, want not,' said the huge, hairy dog, lapping the milk up.

I pressed my body against the counter and began to inch my way to the door, with my phone in my hand. 'You … you …'

The dog made a movement that seemed somewhat like a shrug. 'Yeah. We weren't supposed to meet like this just yet. Thought you'd sleep a bit longer, to be honest.'

'You ... you ...' I scrolled through my numbers, cursing myself. Which number had Max texted me from? What would I say anyway? *'Oh, you know you were saying a stray dog got in? Yeah, well he's here again and ... he talks.'*

'Dogs don't speak,' I said out loud. Of course, I knew that wasn't *quite* true. I knew that there were many dogs who could, and did, talk. Just never, ever, to me.

He shook his head. 'No. No, dogs don't speak. You're absolutely right.'

I made my way to the door, only to find it locked. Perfect. The shower, the slippers, and the lovely night's sleep had lulled me into a false sense of security, and I'd forgotten one very important detail: I still had no keys.

So I did what anyone in my position would do. I began to incant. So what if it wouldn't work? The dog didn't know that, did he?

'I order this door–'

'Leaving so soon?' The dog interrupted me, baring his teeth into something suspiciously close to a sarcastic grin. 'That's a pity. I hoped we could get to know one another better. Seeing as I happen to be your familiar.'

I shook my head, abandoning all thoughts of incantation. 'No. No you're not. Wayfairs don't *have* dog familiars. We have cats. And ...' I let my sentence trail off, not quite willing to say the sad truth out loud: I never had – and most likely never *would* have – a familiar of my own.

He made a shrugging movement again. 'You know what they say, Wanda. You don't choose your familiar.

Your familiar chooses you. Anyway, hadn't you better go? You'll be late for your first day at work.'

'I ... how ...'

'Familiars make it their business to find out everything they can about their witches,' he said in a mock-spooky voice. 'Now begone, if you must. Oh, and there's a spare set of keys by the front door. In the little container on the table shaped like a bone. Like I said, familiars know all.'

I backed out the kitchen door, found the keys, and left the house.

3.And Other Stuff…

By now, you might be wondering a few things about me. Like, why did she bother beginning to incant when it was never going to work? I was wondering the same myself. Incantations have never worked for me. No sort of spell or charm ever has. Yes, I am a witch called Wanda. But I'd be better off being a fish.

Most witches come into their power at five or six. There are some late starters, but very few. Basically if a witch doesn't get their power by twenty-one, they never will.

And you might have noticed, due to the fact that the enchanting Will Berry had mentioned this very fact: I would be turning twenty-one in three days' time.

≈

Okay, I'll admit it, I was a little bit breathless by the time I arrived at Berrys' Bottlers. And not just because I was carrying three bags.

As I veered into the carpark, the front door of the building swung open to reveal Will, in all his glory. Okay, so he was fully clothed, but a girl can dream.

'Bright and early.' He beamed out at me. 'That's what we like to see.' His perfectly chiselled features looked suddenly troubled. He stepped out with a shaking head and, taking my bags from my hands he said, 'That's way too much for you to carry by yourself.'

For the second time since meeting Will, my mind was running in two completely different directions. The modern me wanted to roll my eyes and take my bags out of his hands. The old-fashioned, girly me wanted to swoon at his chivalry.

'Why so many bags, anyway? Is everything all right? Anything I can help you with?'

'Oh, everything's fine,' I replied. 'I've just moved into a new place. I went to collect my stuff before work so I could just go straight home afterwards.'

'Ah.' He smiled. 'New job. New house. It's all change for you. It's not too far from work, is it? I hate to think of you having a long commute.'

'Westerly Crescent. I hadn't heard of it till yesterday, but it turns out it's just a short bus ride from here.'

His eyes rounded. '*Westerly*? In Luna Park?'

'Why? Have you heard something bad about the area?' I sighed. 'Well, there've already been quite a lot of signs that it's too good to be true.'

He gave me a look I couldn't quite fathom. 'I haven't heard anything bad about it, as such. It's nice enough as these places go. And I'm just across the park as a matter of fact. Easterly Crescent is my neighbourhood.'

He led the way through a sparklingly clean production area. Huge vats were chugging away – presumably an automated process – and a conveyer belt sent bottles to be filled, capped and labelled at a fast pace. This didn't look like a factory in the aftermath of a burglary. I wondered what exactly had been stolen.

He plucked a bottle from the line and tossed it to me. 'Have a taste. Aunt Alice's recipe. That's what the thieves stole yesterday, as a matter-of-fact. Luckily, Aunt Alice knows this recipe like the back of her hand.'

I ignored the fact that he seemed to have read my mind (because if he had, surely it just meant we were a perfect match) and eyed the label on the bottle. 'Berry Good Go Juice.' I grinned madly. 'Oh my God, I just had one yesterday. Geez, no wonder someone wanted to nick the recipe. This stuff is *gorgeous!'*

'Nice to hear it,' came a woman's voice.

I turned at the sound and saw a woman of fifty or so, elegantly dressed with stunning blonde hair and light green eyes, walking down from the upstairs offices. I recognised her as the same woman who'd been answering the Gardaí's questions the day before.

'This is Aunt Alice.' William led me towards the woman. 'Auntie, this is our new girl. She'll be doing the accounts on Wednesdays and Fridays, and other stuff with you during the rest of the week.'

She gave me a wide smile, but it didn't manage to meet her eyes. 'So nice to meet you. As long as you like hard work, we'll get along just fine. And what do they call you?'

'Wanda,' I replied. 'Wanda Wayfair. I'm really looking forward to this, Alice. It definitely beats packing shelves at Bargain Bites – that's the supermarket where I used to work.' I was about half way through my nervous word-vomit when I noticed her face change into a scowl.

She turned to Will. 'A word, if you please.'

He cleared his throat. 'Yes. I thought you might say that.' He patted my arm and followed her up the stairs. 'I'll pop your bags into the locker room for you,' he said over his shoulder. 'Go and get yourself a coffee and a muffin, Wanda. Canteen's to your left.'

I decided not to stress about why Aunt Alice had taken a dislike to me. She'd have plenty of time to get to know me, and by the time she was holding Will's and my first-born in her arms, she was sure to be my very best friend.

I wandered into a large canteen area, where a full coffee pot was sitting on a warmer, next to a basket filled with chocolate muffins. My stomach was far too nervous for food – again, absolutely *nothing* to do with Will Berry – so I poured myself a coffee and sat down. Over the next few minutes other workers arrived, digging into muffins and grabbing drinks, chatting easily. They were nice and friendly, but moved quickly off to their work areas, leaving me alone once again.

At one stage I thought I heard furious shouting from somewhere above – from a voice that sounded like Alice's. A moment after that, it all seemed to quieten down. I was on my second cup of coffee when Alice arrived in the canteen, her smile back in place.

'So sorry about that, Wanda. It was a bit of a misunderstanding on my part, but Will's explained it all now.' She sat down across from me and lowered her voice. 'The staff don't know what we are, so this is between you and me. I told Will what I *always* tell him when we need a new accounts and stuff assistant – hire a human for the goddess's sake. But for some reason, this time he decided he knew best. I mean, there's driving involved. *Obviously* I'd prefer not to hire a witch.'

'Oh.' I tried to stop myself from reddening. 'Obviously.'

'But then he told me you're just an Unempowered. So it's all worked out all right, in the end.' She stood up. 'Well, we'd better get going. We have a busy day ahead.'

≈

I pulled out of the carpark, Alice in the seat beside me, jotting things down on a notepad. Once she'd told me where to go, she was too busy to speak. Which suited me fine. As an unempowered witch, I'd spent my whole childhood feeling ostracized. I'd run from my coven as soon as I turned seventeen, and had done my very best every day since to avoid anything supernatural. And it was all going quite well until this morning. Inwardly I said about a dozen swearwords. Outwardly I kept my amiable smile plastered on. I mean, Berrys' Bottlers was in a human enclave for goodness sake. How was I to know it was run by witches?

I quelled a few more silent swears. If something looks too good to be true, it usually is. And Will Berry was the perfect example. The Wayfair name was famous among witches, so there was no way he hadn't known who I was during that interview. He knew who I was, and what I was. I wish I'd had the same privilege.

And he'd lied to me about why his aunt wasn't driving. Stubbed her toe indeed. He'd obviously been trying to hide the fact that he and Alice were witches for as long as possible. *Why* he would have wanted to hide it, though … that was what I didn't understand.

Most witches didn't drive. Not that they couldn't. Just that they didn't. A lot of them seemed to think it was beneath them. I mean why drive when you could snap your fingers and send yourself halfway across the world? Why drive when you could fly a broom, or take a potion?

When in the human world, they usually had chauffeurs. Humans, more often than not. But sometimes they hired unempowered witches like me. That way they could do all the magic they liked in their comfy back seat, while the schmuck up the front kept the car on the road.

Today, I was that schmuck.

I felt Alice looking at me, and I cast a glance in her direction. I'd been right. She *was* looking at me. And she was doing so with an incredibly patronising grin.

'I almost envy you, Wanda. You have the best of both worlds, don't you? Why, driving about, playing about with computers and thingimibobs … you're almost like a human. Or a wizard. Have you ever considered wizardry?'

I did my best not to grunt. These days, a lot of unempowered witches turned to wizardry. That way, they could learn to harness power without actually having any.

'Oh no, never even thought about it,' I lied. I had thought about it. A lot. So much so that I'd secretly studied the art for five years of my teenage-hood before realising: not only did I not *have* any magic; I couldn't even fake it.

She looked at me a little more carefully. 'Do you see your coven often, Wanda?'

I reinforced my smile. I'd need scaffolding to keep my lips in the right place before long. 'Not really. Family events and things. Truth be told, I really enjoy my life here in the human enclaves.'

'Oh, well … I suppose it's probably easier. Too much time around *real* witches might make you bitter. Well, here we are. Take the next right and pull up at the first shop you see.'

≈

Over the course of the day I discovered exactly what *other stuff* my job entailed. I drove Alice to a seemingly endless amount of shops and warehouses. Sometimes we dropped off small crates of Berry Good Go Juice. At other times she gave her sales pitch to the buyers, while I handed her pens and papers and whatever else she couldn't manage to find for herself. It should have been the most boring of days. But after stacking shelves every day and studying accounting every evening for the past four years, it was actually … not that bad. If I could have taken Alice out of the equation, I might have even enjoyed myself.

One interesting thing did happen, though. You know, if you consider a horrific nightmare that you can't look away from to be interesting.

Alice and I stopped for lunch in a pub just off Grafton Street. As lunches go, it was unremarkable. I had a ploughman's, while she had a roast beef sandwich. I drank orange juice. She drank three glasses of red wine. So far, so dull. But just as I was finishing my drink, an odd tingling crept up the back of my spine. I turned around to see a tall man entering the pub. He was wearing a black coat, black hat, black sunglasses, black scarf … well, you get the picture. He was wearing a lot of black. In June. I could see very little of his face, but I guessed he was in his late forties, perhaps early fifties.

While I was still looking in his direction, he disappeared. Honest to the goddess, he just vanished from in front of my eyes. A few seconds later, Alice ordered another drink and I excused myself and went to the loo. Unfortunately, quite a few other ladies seemed to be on the same pee schedule. The queue was out the door. But I'd been to that particular pub before, and I knew there was another ladies' room, down in the basement.

I did what I had to do and, just as I was making my way back up the stairs, I saw the man in black again. He was at the back of a little alcove beneath the staircase, but he wasn't alone. He and Alice were together – *very* much together. It was horrible, and yet I could barely pull my eyes away.

I ran up the stairs, finished what was left of my juice, and played games on my phone. A *lot* of games. When Alice finally came to join me a half hour later, she said nothing about the man and, seeing as I wished I could wipe all memory of it from my mind (does it hurt to scrub your eyeballs?) I said nothing, either. I didn't even mention that two of her blouse buttons were undone. Nice of me, wasn't it?

We spent the afternoon in much the same painful fashion as we had spent the morning. When we returned to the factory, Will was already gone. While Alice spoke briefly with some of the production staff, my phone beeped. I unlocked it to find a short message from Will:

Your bags are in locker number nine. Code is 333. Change it to whatever you like.

I closed the message and walked sullenly towards the locker room. The message had seemed curt, considering how friendly Will had been so far. Maybe the argument with his aunt had made him reconsider his decision to hire me. Even though I was a little confused about why he'd not been completely upfront when hiring me, I definitely didn't want to lose this job. I'd sent out hundreds of CVs, but it seemed there was an overabundance of accountants in Dublin, and Berrys' Bottlers had been the only interview I'd landed. If I lost this job it was back to stacking shelves for half the money.

I walked towards locker nine and punched the code in. As the locker snapped open, my face lit up. Along with my bags there was a large bottle of champagne, a box of chocolates and a card. I opened it eagerly, and read:

Got called out on an unexpected errand. So sorry I can't be there to see how your first day went. But if Aunt Alice was her usual self, then I hope the champers and choccie will be enough to keep you here. Oh, and sorry I didn't tell you we were you-know-whats. I was afraid you wouldn't take the job. Forgive me?

'Best person for the job my behind,' muttered a voice behind me. I turned just in time to see Alice stalking from the room.

4.Home Sweet Home

I had hoped to have another go in the shower before I confronted my coven. Such was not to be. As soon as I turned the Berrys' Bottlers van onto Westerly Crescent, my mother was waiting at the front door of Number One.

I pulled up in the drive, got out of the van and made my way through the weedy garden.

My mother's name was Beatrice Wayfair, and she looked like an older version of myself. Unlike many other witches, she eschewed anti-aging glamours, and so she gave me quite an idea of what I might look like in the future. Her curvy hips were just a *little* curvier than mine. Her heart-shaped face bore only a few smile lines around her warm brown eyes. Her chestnut-coloured hair was neither dyed nor glamoured, and – at forty-five – she had only a few greys peeking through.

The suddenly-overgrown garden might seem strange, I suppose, if you weren't accustomed to the ways of my coven. The Wayfairs, you see, rarely settled in the witch enclaves. They chose, instead, to move around in the human areas. My mother said that living close to humans was a good way to keep the coven down to earth. The Wayfairs were responsible for bringing wayward witches back into line. And how could they be trusted to notice someone overdoing things if they were too busy enjoying the trappings of the witch lifestyle?

Well, that was the official story. The real truth, the truth that I wasn't supposed to know, was that their lifestyle was all because of me. Not having any power, I could only access witch enclaves if I wore my Pendant of Privilege. And I certainly couldn't go to school with other witches. So my family stayed in human areas, growing their garden wild to discourage too many human visitors. If you ever see an overgrown garden, by the way, take it as a sure sign that a witch lives there.

Part of me was grateful that they made so many concessions for me. A much, much larger part of me hated it, because it was just one of the many ways in which they reminded me that I'd never really be one of them.

Sometimes, love hurts. That day, all I wanted to do was rush into my mother's arms. But years of stubbornness, of pretending that I didn't really want to be a proper witch … it weighed on me. It made it difficult to spend time with my coven, let alone tell them how much I loved them and missed them.

But just as I was about to swallow my pride and hug her, my mother narrowed her eyes, put her hands back by her side and glared at the van I'd parked in her drive.

'Berrys' Bottlers?' She raised a curious brow at me. '*That's* your new job?'

'Nice to see you too.'

'Oh, Wanda!' She put her arms out again and pulled me tight. 'It's the best thing in the *world* to see you again. I was just surprised, that's all. But … you do know that the Berrys are witches, right?'

'Yip,' I said through a mouthful of woolly cardigan. Did I mention that my mother's hugs are rather enthusiastic? 'I do now.' I sniffed the air. 'Is that apple tart I smell?'

She laughed. 'You could smell an apple tart from the other side of Ireland, I'll bet.'

She pulled away and pushed me inside. As we entered the old familiar hallway, something else familiar wrapped his way around my ankles. It was Mischief, a tabby tomcat, my mother's familiar. He jumped up into my arms, and I snuggled him tight.

Normally, familiars do *not* like to be petted. But for me, Mischief always made an exception. If it was because he pitied the fact that I would never be a real coven member, well, I didn't care.

Oh, yes, I did say *the old familiar hallway,* didn't I? Well, that's because it was. On the outside, my coven's house might look like it was Number One, Westerly Crescent. No matter where they lived, they always made sure the façade matched the other houses on the road. But inside, now *that* was a different story altogether.

While it might seem like I was walking into my coven's latest rental, I was actually walking into the same house I was born in: the large, rambling house called Wayfarers' Rest. The *real* Wayfarers' Rest was still in Riddler's Cove, a witch enclave on the south-west coast.

I passed by the usual photos on the wall. There were rows of my coven's achievements – the wayward witches they caught and brought to justice, and the Magical Law degrees of all of the Wayfair women. There were photos of me as a child, in my parents' arms. There were photos of my father on his own, winning awards for broom making and flying competitions. There was the photo I loved and avoided in equal measures – of his last day alive, posing with his latest broom design at the foot of Mount Everest, before the competition that killed him.

And then there was the biggest picture of all. Not a photo, but a portrait of the original Wanda the Wayfarer, my namesake. A namesake of which I was undeserved. The first Wanda had been the one who began the Wayfairs' foray into magical law. She'd wandered from place to place (hence the name Wayfarer, which morphed over the years into Wayfair) tracking down wayward witches and supernaturals and bringing them to justice. Her exact powers were unknown, but according to legend she had too many powers to count. She was revered by witches far and wide, and brought about a golden age for all supernatural beings. An age in which she and her kin made sure that the world was a happy and safe place for all.

Or so the legend went. If there really *had* been a golden age, the history books hid it well. And as I entered our large, cosy kitchen behind my mother, I knew that even if there had ever been a golden age for the Wayfairs, it was long, *long* in the past.

Christine sat on the opposite end of the oak table, a scrying bow before her, her long auburn hair hiding whatever vision she might be seeing. Her daughter, Melissa, sat next to her, a Magical Law book open in front of her.

There was no one else in the room. Because these days, there were no more Wayfairs. These days, upholding the law was done mainly by the Wyrd Court's Peacemakers. Wayfairs had jurisdiction over witches, only. The Wyrd Court's Peacemakers were in charge of every other supernatural criminal. Very few witches wanted to be part of a coven with so little sway, and no one new had joined our coven for years.

Melissa looked up from her law book, her green eyes widening in joy. She rushed from the table and squeezed me almost as tightly as my mother had done. Mischief jumped out of my arms just in time and settled in his basket in front of the wood-burning stove. Christine soon joined in with the hugging, and my mother went to the oven to take out the apple tart.

By the time I finally managed to pull away and catch my breath, a large plate of apple tart was on the table, with ice cream melting on top.

I suppressed my drooling just long enough to take a seat. 'Oh my stars,' I said between mouthfuls. 'It's been soooo long since I had anything this good.'

Christine smiled at me, placing a brimming mug of tea next to my plate. 'Well, you know how you can remedy that,' she said with a wink. 'Visit us more often.'

In the chair beside me, Melissa was talking ten to the dozen about her Magical Law course, about how amazing Crooked College was, about how lovely and smart and *blah*

blah blah all of the guys there were. Okay, so the whole *blah blah blah* thing might have sounded just a tad on the bitter side. But that's the thing – no matter how much I wished otherwise, I *was* bitter. When I was still young enough to think I'd get my power, I'd wanted to go to Crooked College more than anything in the world.

Melissa was my age. Christine and my mother had both been pregnant at the same time, and Melissa and I were born just days apart. Like her mother, Melissa looked every inch the beautiful witch. They shared the same long auburn hair and green eyes. You could easily mistake them for sisters because, unlike my own mother, Christine *did* use anti-aging glamours. Quite a lot of them.

We weren't related, other than through our coven. Their actual surname was Brady, and their line was relatively new to magic, their power only going back a century or so. They could have formed their own coven. Every witch family had that right. But it was common for smaller lines like the Bradys' to join the coven of a larger, more established witch family. Not that the Wayfair coven could be considered large these days. Seeing as I was useless in any magical regard, without Christine and Melissa, my mother would be the only Wayfair left.

Christine tousled my hair and returned to her scrying bowl. 'Excuse my rudeness,' she said through a curtain of hair. 'But things are happening. Big things. I need to keep an eye on the action.'

At the moment she was viewing through a bowl filled with water, but Christine could use *anything* for her visions. Crystal balls, flames, mirrors … you name it.

Some witches were of the belief that scrying bowls could only be used to see into other worlds. Christine knew better. She saw other worlds, yes. But she also saw this one. The future *and* the present. Her visions were far from perfect, but they certainly helped with investigations.

'Big things?' I looked at my mother, then shook my head. 'Never mind. Nothing to do with me.'

She took a seat opposite me, sipping at a mug of tea. 'None of that talk now, Wanda. It's only Tuesday, after all. Anything could happen before your birthday on Friday.'

'Sure,' I scoffed. 'Though if my Monday and Tuesday are anything to go by, then I sincerely doubt that it'll be anything good.'

She reached out and grasped my hand, a look of concern on her heart-shaped face. 'It's not that Alice Berry, is it? I've had the displeasure of meeting that woman before. So if she's giving you a hard time, you've only to say.'

I snorted. My mother had quite the way of dealing with all of my childhood bullies. Little girls and boys who teased me for being unempowered soon found themselves with boils in uncomfortable places. I could just imagine what she might do to Alice Berry. 'Alice is fine,' I said. 'I doubt we'll be bosom buddies but … she's okay.'

'So what's the matter? What's been so bad about this week?'

I chewed at my lip. Where would I begin? More to the point, *would* I begin at all? I hadn't seen my mother face to face for a very long time. Although the urge to pour my misery upon her was strong, I wondered if I should resist. I mean, it was hardly fair, was it? Say nothing to her for months and, when I finally do open my mouth, do nothing but carp and moan?

'Oh, nothing really,' I said eventually. 'Just … y'know. New job. And my old house had mould, apparently, so I had to move. Been a bit of a weird week. But like you say, it's only Tuesday.' I forced a smile. 'Things can only get better, eh?'

Instead of congratulating me for my oh-so-sunny disposition, my mother was carefully studying her mug of tea. 'Well.' She cleared her throat. 'Some of that *might* be down to me. Just a very tiny bit. Infinitesimal, really.'

I widened my eyes. If the apple tart weren't so nice, I might have huffily pushed it away and refused to eat another bite. But I never did have the courage of my convictions. 'What do you mean?' I asked through a mouthful of pastry and ice cream. 'Which parts, exactly, were down to you?'

Melissa had long stopped attempting to study. She picked her book up and said, 'I have to, em …do … something,' gave me a quick squeeze of the shoulder, and ran up to her room.

'Well, you can't really blame me, can you?' my mother pleaded. 'I mean, what with these murders and everything. I thought you'd be safer at the hotel, so I sent a bit of toxic mould your way. Still.' She shrugged. 'Westerly Crescent is an enclave, at least. I knew you'd have sense enough to keep out of the human world as much as you could for the time being.'

I gawped at her, ice cream and crumbs dangling and melting in a very unladylike fashion from the corners of my mouth. I mentioned before that with a name like Wanda, I might as well be a fish? Well, at that moment, I imagine I looked like one, too.

'Where do I ... I mean …' I swallowed the last of my food, but still couldn't unhinge my jaw. 'You … you made my house mouldy. And … murders? What murders? And this is an *enclave*?' I smacked a hand against my forehead. 'Well, duh. Of course it's a bloody enclave.' I groaned. The signs had been so clear that even a *blind* unempowered witch could have seen them. The woman with the sunglasses, pulling her blinds down – well, she was definitely a vampire. And, seeing as she was shutting out the *evening* light instead of the daylight, then she was more than likely a dayturner.

And as for the gadgets I'd seen cutting the lawns and trimming the hedges of the other neighbours, well they'd been far too efficient to have been created in the human world. They were magical devices. Made by witches or, more likely, wizards. Westerly Crescent was a supernatural enclave. The whole of Luna Park was, I imagined. *That* would explain why Will Berry thought it was weird that I didn't know the area. How was he to know that I'd spent all of my life avoiding areas just like this? And Hilltop Hotel? I groaned once again. Well, if my mother sent me there to keep safe, then it was in a supernatural area, too.

'I was a bit worried when you never responded to my texts,' she went on. 'But thank the stars you read them, at least. I mean, I know you don't always wear your pendant, so …' She blinked, peering at my neck. Her eyes narrowed, and she moved closer. 'Open your shirt, Wanda. Show me your neck.'

Too confused to argue, I undid the top few buttons, and my mother gazed at my naked, unadorned neck.

'Christine!' She slapped a hand to her mouth. Then she slapped Christine across the head. Then she slapped a hand to her chest, like she was counting her heartbeats. 'Christine!' she called again.

Christine looked up. The ends of her hair were wet, having strayed into her scrying bowl, and her eyes were a little unfocused. 'What? This better be big, Bea,' she said to my mother. 'Because what I'm looking at in this bowl right now *is.'*

'Look at her neck,' said my mother. 'Just look at her neck.'

Christine's eyes followed my mother's. She slapped a hand across her mouth. She slapped a hand to the table. Finally, she grasped my mother's hand, and the two of them stared at me, tears running down their faces.

'Wanda,' said Christine breathlessly. 'Did you have your pendant on when you went to the hotel?'

I slowly shook my head.

'And you went there on your own?' she pressed. 'No problems finding it?'

I will admit, here and now, that the past few days hadn't displayed me in my best light. You'd be forgiven if, by now, you had me pegged as a little bit thick. I'd overlooked *many* important facts. I'd paid attention to nothing but where I was going to live and where I was going to work. And – ahem – perhaps I'd paid just a *little* bit of attention to how well Will Berry could fill out his shirt. But, in the interest of retaining *some* self-esteem, let's just say that it wasn't *all* my fault. I mean, I'd lived in the human world and avoided the magical one for such a long time. I hardly expected it to come thundering back in, did I?

I never wore my Pendant of Privilege these days. Why would I? I donned it when I went to visit my family at Riddler's Cove for the Winter Solstice, and that was about it. I wore it a little more often when I was a child, because we often travelled to witch enclaves for my father's competitions. But I didn't *want* to travel into the magical enclaves any more than I had to. I didn't need any more reminders of just how un-magical I was, thank you very much. And, although my mother had tried to educate me on Dublin's supernatural enclaves when I moved here, I hadn't listened to a word.

Here's the thing about the enclaves. Even an unempowered witch – me – could enter many of the supernatural enclaves as and when I liked. Despite my lack of power, the wards that were erected around the areas (spells that protected the area from outsiders) could sense that I was still supernatural. As long as I knew where somewhere like Westerly Crescent was situated, I could find my way there. And Max's directions had shown me the way.

But to enter a *witch* enclave … that was a whole different story. Witch enclaves were for witches only. And by witches, I mean real witches. Ones that can put warts up your nostrils and hairs on your eyeballs sort of witches. Oh, where I was living now – in a place that was no doubt supernatural – *that* wasn't the big deal. It was where I'd visited yesterday afternoon and again this morning that was so amazing. Because now that I no longer had my head stuck up my behind, I knew for certain: the Hilltop Hotel was a witches' hotel. The whole of Warren Lane could well be a witch enclave for all I knew. I'd never been to the place before yesterday. For an unempowered witch, gaining entry without a Pendant of Privilege simply shouldn't be possible.

I swallowed a mouthful of saliva, followed it with a mouthful of tea and then stuttered, 'So is W-Warren Lane a witch enclave? And if it is w-well w-what d-does that m-mean?'

I knew what it meant. Scratch that – I knew what I *hoped* it meant. But after all these years of pretending not to care about being unempowered … I was suddenly afraid to hope that anything otherwise could be possible.

'It means,' said Christine, unable to keep the smile from her face, 'that you've come into your power.'

My mother came across to hug me. Christine joined in and, no longer needing to pretend she wasn't listening to every word we'd been saying, Melissa thundered down the stairs to hug me, too.

When they eventually let me up for air I said, a little too nonchalantly, 'Well … I never for a minute doubted it would happen. And also …' A memory of that morning's encounter rushed to the fore. 'I already knew. Because I met my familiar this morning. And he's a dog.'

'A dog!' my mother exclaimed. 'Why, we've not had a dog familiar in the coven for generations. Where is he? What's his name? Why didn't you tell me sooner? What–?'

Christine shook her head and squeezed my mother's arm. 'Sorry to interrupt. But in the excitement, I almost forgot what I was about to show you.' Her face was pained as she pulled my mother and Melissa to the scrying bowl. 'You can come too, Wanda. I'll be able to let you into the vision, now you're empowered. I only wish that your first vision could be a nicer one. Come on everyone. Come quick.'

Wondering what I was about to see, I gathered with the others around the bowl. As far as scrying bowls went, Christine's were as beautiful as they were simple. This particular one was made of rowan, with a crystal star at the bottom, and moons and suns carved about the edges. Until today, I'd never been able to see anything but the bowl itself.

Christine could freeze important visions when she found them, in order to let other witches catch a glimpse of what she'd seen in her bowl. And what she'd seen today made my blood run cold.

A tiny, skinny old woman was lying beside a duck pond in St Stephen's Green. Half of a tennis racket – the top part – was lying by her side. The other part – the handle of the racket – was embedded in the old woman's stomach.

She was dead. There was no doubt about it. A few feet away, a park warden was holding back a young man who was dressed in tennis whites.

'I dunno why I done it,' the young man frantically shouted. 'I swear. You have to believe me. I dunno why I done it.'

My mother's face paled. 'We have to get there, and we have to get there now,' she said. 'I know that poor woman. I mean … I *knew* that poor woman'

'So did I,' I said sadly, looking down at the frail, dead form on the ground. The woman in Christine's vision was Maureen O'Mara.

5.At the Click of a Finger

It could take years to learn the art of finger-clicking, and we didn't have years. So I did as I used to when I was a child. I held tight to my mother's hand, and travelled as her passenger.

No sooner had her fingers struck together than we were there – well, nearly there.

On a bright and sunny June day such as this one, it would hardly have been a good idea to appear in the middle of St Stephen's Green. It was all very well to say that people might not notice. After all, they had a murder to distract their attention. But this was hardly the time to take a risk, so instead my mother, Christine, Melissa and I travelled to a carpark in the shopping centre directly across the road from the park. It was dark in there, and no one noticed us.

We ran quickly out of the carpark, through the shopping centre and across the road. As we went, my mother filled me in on what had been happening.

The article *In Dublin's Scare City* had only half the story, it seemed. Yes, there had been a recent spate of attacks in Dublin. But so far, all of the victims had been witches.

'And the weird thing is,' said Melissa breathlessly as we ran towards the duck pond, 'that all of the people *doing* the attacking have been humans.' Melissa realised what she said, laughed a little and rolled her eyes. 'Okay, so *maybe* there's a little bit of a history with humans murdering witches. But trust me, Wanda. This is different.'

As we neared the pond, I clutched my stomach. I thought my years of shelf-stacking and walking everywhere had kept me fit. But running to a murder scene, it appeared, took a whole new level of fitness. My mother and Christine seemed barely fazed. Melissa, thankfully, looked a little red about the face. What? I wasn't glad that she looked slightly less perfect than usual. I'm *not* that sort of girl.

'So the murder across the road from my old house … that victim was a witch?'

Melissa nodded. 'But his girlfriend was human. His name was Eoin Reynolds. He was a few years ahead of me in Crooked College. He just graduated the year before last and got appointed to the Department of Magical Law at the Wyrd Court. Junior Clerk. Even with all of the new work he had to do, he still found time to come back to the college and visit his friends there. I met Susanne plenty of times – his girlfriend. I could only ever meet her in the human enclaves, obviously. Lovely, she was. Not a bad bone in her body. And she was mad about him, too.'

I thought of the girl I'd seen the day before, being shoved into the garda car. She'd seemed shocked at what she'd done. Just like the young man in Christine's vision.

'Damn it!' My mother gritted her teeth. An ambulance was rushing through the park, on its way out. There were hundreds of people milling around the pond, being pushed back by the gardaí while crime scene tape was being erected. There were journalists by the dozens. 'Too many people. We can't freeze time now. It'll be way too much to fix afterwards.'

Christine nodded reluctantly. 'You're right. We'll have to come back when it's dark. We can travel straight into the park when it's closed for the night. Even if there are a few gardaí around, it won't be too much of a fix.'

'But will we find anything?' Melissa asked worriedly. 'I mean, all of the evidence will have been taken away by then, won't it?'

'What about that garda friend of yours?' I asked my mother. 'Wouldn't we be better off asking him?'

'We might be,' my mother replied with a sad frown, 'if he hadn't died of a heart attack two weeks ago.' She squeezed my hand. 'But you're right. He would have been a much better option than trying to find evidence amongst all of this mess.'

I didn't know quite what to say. Garda Detective O'Moore had been more than just a contact for my mother. He'd been a friend. And amongst all of these recent crimes, the fact that one of the healthiest men I knew had suddenly died of a heart attack seemed ever-so-slightly suspicious. But no doubt my mother had already thought of that.

We watched in frustrated silence as the gardaí led the young murderer towards a car. Another garda walked alongside, a bottle in his hands.

'At least let me have me drink back,' the murderer pleaded. 'It's bleedin' roastin' today.'

The garda grunted, unscrewed the cap and sniffed the bottle. 'Suppose so,' he said, handing the drink back to the young man. 'Can't smell any alcohol in it.'

'There could be drugs in it though, Ed,' the female garda said through clenched teeth.

Ed rolled his eyes. 'Fine,' he said with a sigh and snatched the bottle back. 'Miss Smarty-Pants Siobhan always knows best.'

As my mother, Christine and Melissa turned away from the scene, I narrowed my eyes and examined the bottle. It was, undoubtedly, a very delicious drink, and one made by the company I'd just begun working for.

'Don't suppose you have any more of the crime scene visions frozen, have you?' I said to Christine as we made our way back to the carpark.

'I do, as a matter of fact. I take recordings of the important visions so we can look at them as and when we need to. Why?' She could barely hide the grin on her face, and my mother was just the same. 'You … you *want* to help us?'

At the sight of their hopeful faces, a guilty weight formed in my stomach. All of these years, they'd done their best to include me. They'd assured me, time and again, that I could still be a useful Wayfair, power or not. And time and again I'd turned them down. Maybe it was time to stop feeling sorry for myself. Maybe it was time to offer them whatever help I could.

6.Frozen Stare

I tried not to grin like a child who's just been told that everything in the sweet shop is free. But it was hard to play it cool when Christine was taking the most amazing ice-tray out of the freezer.

'She doesn't even *need* to keep them in the freezer,' Melissa told me with a roll of her eyes. 'Mam could freeze an entire desert if she wanted to. She just keeps them in ice-cube trays because she thinks it's funny.'

'It is funny,' Christine countered.

'Yeah. Hilarious.' Melissa looked at me. 'Whatever you do, do *not* put the wrong ice-cube in your drink. That's all I'm saying.'

'If you want to be a Wayfair, then you'd better be vigilant.' Christine gave her daughter a wicked grin. 'I'm just making sure you *always* keep your eye on the details. Anyway … I call these my Frozen Stares. Envisioning is, unfortunately, an imperfect art. And where there are this many attacks so close together, it's even more difficult to see everything. I have no visions of Connor Cramer or Adeline Albright, unfortunately.'

I recalled both names from *In Dublin's Scare City*. 'Connor was the guy who was attacked with the candlestick, and Adeline was the one who got away, right?'

'Connor's candles were amazing,' said my mother. 'He'll be missed. Luckily, poor Adeline managed to escape *her* attacker. She's librarian at Crooked College, and a pretty important chronicler to boot.'

The sections in the ice-cube tray were formed into snowflakes. After examining the tray a moment, Christine popped out the one she needed and took it to the scrying bowl. As the Frozen Stare melted in the water, a vision appeared.

It was the sitting room of the house across the road from my old one. Susanne Clemens sat on the couch next to a young, chubby male witch.

'That's Eoin,' Melissa said sadly.

I recognised him, just vaguely. I'd seen him go in and out of the house, though I'd never paid him much attention. I never would have guessed he was a witch. But then, I didn't have the power to sense such things. Now, looking at the vision of the two of them together, contentedly watching TV, I had the sudden sense of knowing. I *knew* he was a witch in the same way I knew Susanne was not. There was a certain tingle I felt when looking at poor, deceased Eoin, as though I could feel his power, even though I was merely looking at him via a vision.

As we watched, Susanne began to scratch her ear furiously. A moment later, her eyes grew cloudy. She drained the last of the bottle she'd been drinking from – my stomach churned when I saw that it was, as I feared, a bottle of Berry Good Go Juice – and then turned to look at her boyfriend with a dazed look in her eyes. She plonked the empty bottle onto the table next to her, picked up a crystal vase filled with flowers, and smashed it over Eoin's head.

Ice-cube after ice-cube revealed the same as the Frozen Stare of Eoin's murder. In every single vision, there was a bottle of Berry Good Go Juice. Either in the hands of the attacker, or close-by. Very few of the victims managed to get away. Unfortunately, Christine didn't have visions of all of the attacks, but what she did have painted a *very* suspicious picture.

'Well.' Melissa shrugged her shoulders. 'I suppose it *could* be a coincidence. The stuff is popular. Everyone's drinking it these days. I mean, have you tasted it?'

'I certainly have,' my mother growled. 'And I tell you this much. Delicious though it may be, *none* of us will be drinking it after this.' She looked at me. 'Now, technically, we're not supposed to be looking at these murder scenes. None of us. The Wyrd Court are investigating. Justine Plimpton – the Minister for Magical Law – she says that because it's humans carrying out the killings, it's nothing to do with the Wayfairs.'

'We've put in a gazillion requests, but Justine's department insists that we have to stick to witches,' Melissa added, passing me a glass of orange juice. It warmed me that she remembered it was my favourite drink. 'But *we* think they just want to phase out Wayfairs altogether, so their Peacemakers can be the only enforcers of Magical Law. In this case, Justine's being especially stubborn.

There's obviously a witch behind this. She'd rather screw the Wayfairs out of a warrant than save lives.'

'And now with *this*.' Christine nodded her head to the latest Frozen Stare that was playing in her scrying bowl. A woman in a business-suit was gulping down some Berry Good Go juice, before scratching her ear, removing her stiletto, and stabbing a victim through the eye. 'We certainly have reason to think that the Berrys might be involved. I mean, it *is* the Berrys, after all. When have any of that lot been angels?'

I took a sip of my juice, feeling my face grow hot. I knew nothing about the Berrys, or about most of the witch covens other than my own. I suddenly regretted all the years of ignoring that side of my life. 'So … are *all* the Berrys a bit dodgy? The receptionist at the hotel seemed impressed that I was working for them.'

My mother snorted. 'Yes. Well. Money and power do have that effect on some people.' She stood up. 'I'm going to go and buy a bottle of that stuff. I don't care *what* the Wyrd Court says. There *is* a witch behind all of this, and I'm going to find out who.' She snapped her fingers, and disappeared.

≈

While my mother was gone, the rest of us began to cook dinner. Even though I rarely came back to my old kitchen, I moved around the place easily. Melissa's and Christine's familiars – both black cats, a mother and daughter called Queenie and Princess – appeared at one point, meowing for their dinner. As soon as they were fed, they joined Mischief in the bed by the wood-burner, and completely ignored us.

Cat rudeness aside, it was all so lovely that it nearly brought tears to my eyes. But there was no point in crying over wasted years. I'd just have to make sure I never let my stubbornness get in my own way again.

By the time my mother snapped back into the room, a vegetable lasagne was on the table, along with salad, garlic bread and a bottle of red wine.

'Well,' she said, huffing into her seat and pouring herself a glass. 'I'm certainly glad we've got a bottle of *this*. It might just take the edge off the fact that I couldn't manage to buy a bottle of what we really need.'

Christine groaned. 'How can that be?'

'Every single shop was sold out. They all said they'd be getting their next delivery on Thursday morning.'

I nodded. That made sense. Tomorrow I was to work with Mike, the company accountant. Thursday would be my next day spent driving Miss Alice, so no doubt we'd be making the deliveries then. I was just thinking about how much I was *not* looking forward to seeing her again when I sensed six pairs of eyes staring at me. Everyone, including the cats, was looking in my direction.

'Oh.' I poured my own glass of wine. Sometimes, nice though it was, orange juice just wasn't enough. 'You want *me* to get you a bottle, don't you?'

My mother patted my hand. 'I wouldn't ask if we didn't need to test it so badly. Mark my words, if the

Berrys are behind this, they'll be doing their best to make sure I can't get my hands on any.'

'But how will you even test it? None of you are potions' experts.'

'No. But we have one working on our side. Ronnie Plimpton.'

'Plimpton? As in a member of the same coven as *Justine* Plimpton? The minister who apparently hates you guys?'

My mother and Christine shared a wicked grin.

'Let's just say that the Wayfair coven is a *little* bit bigger than appearances might suggest,' said Christine.

'Look, I know you're a little wary of doing this.' My mother fixed her brown eyes on me. Good Gretel, she knew just how to get to me. 'But it has to be you. The Berrys know I don't like them, so they'll probably be expecting me to go snooping. They'll have protections against me. Magic won't be able to get me inside. Only a person who's invited – like you – will be able to gain entry. And also …' She bit her lip and looked at the floor. 'Perhaps it might be better if they *don't* know you've come into your power. Just for now.'

I looked away from her and took a gulp of my wine. Snooping around the factory where I'd *just* been employed. Stealing bottles of juice. Spying on the Berrys. Lying about my newfound power. Could I do it? Will's face crossed my mind. His lovely dimpled cheeks. His dazzling smile. Could he really be a suspect in any of this? I took another gulp of wine and sighed. 'Sure. I'll do whatever it takes.'

With a relieved smile from my mother, we all began to eat. Despite the fact that I'd helped with the cooking, the food was really good. We'd just started on dessert – more apple tart and ice cream – when my mobile rang.

I looked down at the number, not recognising it. 'Hello?' I said after answering.

'Wanda Wayfair?'

'That's me.'

'Ah good. Wanda, this is Sheila Flannery. Receptionist at the Hilltop Hotel. I'm calling because you left something behind.'

'What?' I scrunched up my forehead, trying to think what it could have been. 'I'm sure I have everything. I mean, I didn't even unpack.'

'Well,' Sheila replied with a high-pitched laugh, 'some things don't really need packing, do they. And according to him, he's definitely yours.'

'According to *him?'*

'Yes. Him. Your familiar. He's waiting in the foyer for you. Got his case packed and everything. Shall I tell him you're on your way?'

7.Familiarity Breeds Unkempt

My mother stood beside me. ‘It’s up to you,’ she said. ‘I can hold your hand again, or you can try and do it yourself.’

I bit my lip. ‘I’ve only *just* got my power. Will I be able to travel without you?’

‘Probably not,’ she admitted. ‘But it’s as good an opportunity as any to try. You’ve been at the hotel, so you know it. That’s a good start. It’s *much* easier to travel to places you’re familiar with. All you need to do is picture it in your mind, let the power trickle to your fingertips, then click your fingers. I’ll travel with you, either way. It’s up to you.’

I brought an image of the hotel foyer to mind. That part was easy. But sending the power to my fingertips? I mean, what power? I felt a tingle, I supposed. But it could just as easily have been an itch. Earlier on I’d been able to sense the power in the other witches, while I watched their murders in Christine's Frozen Stares. But sensing power, whilst a beginning, was *just* a beginning.

'Okay,' I said, despite my lack of confidence. 'I'll try.'

I snapped my fingers. I was still in the kitchen. My mother gave me a reassuring smile. 'It's okay, love. There's plenty of time to practise. For now, I'll hold your hand and we'll go and get your dog.'

'Yes,' I said unsurely as she grasped my hand in hers. 'My dog.'

But even before we appeared in the foyer, I had the sneaking suspicion that, although we were definitely going to find my familiar waiting for me, he was *not* going to be a dog.

≈

My mother brought us to a dark corner of the foyer, next to an old pay phone and the men's toilets. It smelled … interesting. So interesting that the two of us ran as fast as we could to the reception desk.

'Ah,' said Sheila, the receptionist. 'You finally came for the poor little fella.'

I got the feeling that she was far from impressed with my having abandoned my familiar. I suddenly noticed something I'd overlooked the first time I met Sheila. The large brooch on her lapel was *not* a simple piece of gaudy, cat-shaped jewellery. That bejewelled cat was stretching out and looking at me through narrowed green eyes. The brooch gave a golden flash, then jumped from her lapel. A furry, fat marmalade cat now stood on top of the reception desk, hissing at me.

Sheila stroked the cat and looked adoringly at it. 'This is my Mr Cuddles,' she said in one of those coochy coo voices. 'Aren't you my Mr Cuddles? Yes, yes you *are* my Mr Cuddles.'

Mr Cuddles hissed once more, and jumped onto the floor.

'You really ought to get yours charmed,' said Sheila, giving me a stern look. 'He could get abandonment issues, you know. If brooches don't take your fancy, you could have your little fella turned into a necklace, a ring … anything. Then you could take him with you anywhere. Even to the human enclaves.'

'Well, I'll think about that,' I replied tonelessly. 'Speaking of my little fella …?'

'Oh, yes. He's right over …' Sheila bit her lip. Her eyes took on a feverish look and she screamed, 'No, Mr Cuddles! No!'

My mother and I followed her terrified gaze. Over by the fireplace, Mr Cuddles was pouncing up onto an armchair. It was facing the fire, so we couldn't see if anyone was occupying it. If they were, they were incredibly small. There was a loud screech, one that very nearly made my ears bleed.

We ran towards the armchair, Sheila at our heels. As we neared the area, we saw Mr Cuddles slinking away from the chair. He had a definite limp, and a bloody mouth. He made straight for Sheila, jumping into her arms and shaking like a pile of fat, furry jelly.

As we finally got to the chair, my eyes widened and my jaw dropped open.

My mother nudged me and whispered, 'I thought you said your familiar was a dog.'

I looked at the small, toothless rat sitting in the armchair. There was a tiny suitcase by his side, and he had an even smaller crossword book open in his lap. He looked up from his puzzle and said with a lisp, 'Ah, there you are, Wanda. About time too. Can we go home now? It's well after my bedtime.'

'I …' I began, eloquently. 'You …' I added, even more eloquently. 'But … I … You …'

'Enlightening though this conversation is, perhaps we could finish it off later.' He extended a tiny hand – or was it a paw? – in my mother's direction. 'I assume you're Goodwitch Wayfair? Very pleased to meet you.'

Though my mother extended a hand and shook his paw, I couldn't help but notice she wrinkled her nose ever so slightly as she did so. It wasn't long before I realised why. As well as having patchy fur and nearly no teeth, the rat also gave off an interesting smell. Interesting, as in disgusting. Maybe that enchanting musk we'd noticed upon arrival hadn't been emanating from the men's loo, after all.

The stench did have one thing going for it, however. It made me feel incredibly alert. Probably a fight or flight response, I surmised, because there was no doubt about it – I wanted to run as far as I could from the creature in the chair. My mind kicked into gear, and I regained the power of speech.

I turned to my mother. 'I was joking about the dog,' I lied. 'I hadn't met my familiar yet. I thought it'd be funny, y'know, to say I had a dog. Because all of the coven have cats.'

'So … not a dog then? And you hadn't met this rat before?'

'Oh, I met him all right. He was here in the hotel toilets while I was getting changed for my interview. But I had *no* idea he was my familiar.' I eyed the rat again, doing my best not to breathe in as I asked him, 'What's your name then, oh familiar of mine?'

He gave me a toothless grin. 'Dudley,' he said. 'And I really wish you'd stop making *me* look like the rude one, Wanda. Because I have to ask you – yet again – can we get the hell out of here?'

'Sure,' I replied weakly. 'Why the hell not?'

≈

The journey back was technically just as fast as the journey there. But this time, it felt a lot longer. Holding a rat with hygiene issues can have that effect.

We reappeared in my mother's kitchen. The three cats, all curled up by the fire, gave Dudley a brief glance before returning to their slumber. They were cleverer than Mr Cuddles then. Though I doubted it would take much.

'Is that really a thing, then?' I asked my mother as I placed Dudley onto a dining chair and went to wash my hands. 'Having your familiar charmed into a piece of jewellery.'

My mother shuddered. ‘It’s the latest fashion. Most familiars would never let you do it to them. I mean, they’re not accessories, are they? And they have their own ways of getting about the place. They certainly don’t need our help.’

‘I saw Veronica Berry wear hers as an enormous ring on TV last week,’ Melissa said.

‘Berry? Any relation to my new employers?’ I wondered.

Melissa shrugged. ‘It’s a massive coven. And like all covens, they all take the same surname, whether they’re related or not. You’ve really never heard of Veronica Berry, have you?’

Dudley snorted. Some sort of yellowish substance came from his nose as he did, and he opened his suitcase, pulled out a box of tissues, and blew his nose. ‘Of course she’s never heard of Veronica Berry. I almost envy you, Wanda. I often wish I could forget some of her performances. *Witches do it Better* ... now that one was particularly bad.’

Melissa and Christine suddenly noticed the new arrival. Christine held a hand above her nose and said, ‘I thought you said your familiar was a *dog*.’

‘Yes. Well. That was a joke,’ I said, repeating my earlier lie. I scooped Dudley up, along with his little case and crossword book. ‘And now I’d better get him home. I have to get up bright and early if I want to get some Berry Good Go Juice without anyone noticing.’

My mother’s face fell. ‘You’re not staying with us?’

My heart ached. My nose also ached, throbbingly so, because Dudley was a lot worse this close at hand. 'All my things are there. And I don't want to let Max down. He's my new housemate and he's been … well, he's been … well, he could have been worse, I suppose. He doesn't seem to write his name on his food, which is a plus point in any house share. Anyway, he could probably do with the rent money.'

All three witches gave me a strange look, glanced at each other and mouthed, 'Money?'

But whatever that was about, it would have to wait. Because I really did need an early night. And before I could slip under the covers, Dudley would need to slip into a bath.

8.Dudley's Witch

I'd come up with all sorts of plans for how I could force Dudley into a bath. But as I filled the sink in my en suite with warm water and bubble bath, it was clear that I needn't have bothered with the internal scheming.

Dudley, who I'd housed on the little chair by the window (a window which I had immediately opened wide), was opening up his case. First, he removed a tiny bar of soap. Next came his scrubbing brush, towel, and a rubber duck.

'I was worried about coming to live with you, but I see I needn't have been,' he called into the bathroom. 'Maureen was right. You're *not* as stupid as you look.'

I goggled at him through the open adjoining door. 'Maureen? O'Mara?'

He gave me a gummy grin. 'Ah, so she *did* get to meet you before she was murdered. She was worried she might not get the chance. She even had the two of us split up so we'd increase our chances of explaining things to you before she got killed. That was very rude of you, by the way. Ignoring me the way you did in the hotel toilets.'

I couldn't decide where to begin. 'Ignoring you? I didn't even hear you, so how could I ignore you?'

Dudley twirled one of his whiskers and glowered at me. 'Liar. I even waved at you to get your attention. And you had your power by then. Only just, but still.'

'Did I? I suppose I must have, seeing as I found my way into a witch enclave without my pendant on. But I really *didn't* hear you. Maybe it's not all coming at once. My power, I mean.' I turned off the tap. Any more water and he'd drown. 'Look, go back a bit. How did you know Maureen O'Mara? And … did *she* know she'd be murdered?'

'Listen, I'm happy to answer all of your questions. That's what I'm here for. But can you please hurry up and get me into my bath? Maureen gave me six a day, you know. So get me in there, and while I give myself a good scrub I'll tell you everything.'

I lifted him into the sink. It would suit us both if he were in pleasant-smelling water while we spoke.

'Maureen was my witch,' he explained as he soaped up his patchy fur. 'That's what she always said. Never that I was her familiar. Always that she was my witch. She understood things, you see, did Maureen. She knew how things really were and she didn't need to fool anyone, including herself. We grew old together. Got dentures together. The whole shebang.' Was that a tear, I wondered, or just a splash of water below his eye? 'Speaking of dentures, you'll need to pick my new ones up. Unless you want me talking through my gums for the rest of our time together.' He had begun to use his scrubbing brush now. Little bits of fur came loose in the water while he worked. It was as fascinating as it was gross.

'You know,' he said while he pushed his rubber ducky with a toe, 'I wanted nothing more than to die with her. That's the usual way, isn't it? Grow old with your witch. Die together. But Maureen wouldn't have it. She said you were the next Wayfarer. That you'd find her murderer and send them to Witchfield. And once I'd helped you do that, then I could finally join her in the afterlife.'

I shuddered. I might have established a certain wilful ignorance when it came to the witching world, but even I knew about our infamous prison, Witchfield. 'Wait. The next Wayfarer? There already *are* Wayfarers. Well, Wayfairs, anyway. My whole coven are Wayfairs.'

'No.' He was soaping himself all over again. I could understand why it would take more than one going over. Already, he was smelling better. Not smelling *good* yet. Just better. 'They're Wayfairs, yes. But not Wayfarers. Not like you. I mean, don't misunderstand me. They're very good at what they do. Your mother, especially, is so good that she's made a *lot* of powerful enemies. But you … well you're like the original Wanda. You already have one of her magical talents. It won't be long before you get the rest.'

'Wanda? As in Wanda the Wayfarer? My ancestor Wanda? My inappropriate namesake, Wanda? How am I like *her?* I mean, how would you even know? No one knows. It's all stories and legends at this stage. No one knows the truth about how she caught so many criminals. It's all lost in the annals of time or whatever.'

'Maureen knew. Some of it, anyway. That was why she wanted to share a room with you. So she could fill you in on it all.'

He was scrubbing again. I thought he couldn't possibly lose any more fur. Apparently I was wrong.

'That makes no sense,' I argued, thinking about the last time I saw Maureen alive. She'd told me to look in the paper. In it, I'd learned about the murders. I'd also found this room at an extremely cheap price. Now that I thought about it, I was sure that there was magic behind me finding this houseshare. A mysterious breeze flipping the paper to *just* the right page? I mean, come on. 'I think Maureen wanted me to live here, Dudley. She didn't *want* me at the hotel.'

'You're right. She helped you find this house. But that was Plan B, so to speak. Plan A was for you to share a room so she could tell you everything. But she had a vision in the hotel, just before you left to catch your bus. She foresaw that she was going to be murdered very soon. So we went our separate ways to try and get your attention – I tried to talk to you in the loo, while Maureen headed for the bus stop. There was never going to be enough time to explain everything, so she did what she thought was most important – she kept you safe.'

He'd run out of soap, and I passed him another tiny bar. 'What do you mean? Keep *me* safe? You said she envisioned *her* murder. Not mine.'

'Yes, but she only knew she was *going* to be killed. She didn't know where. She was afraid it might happen in the hotel room, and that you might get caught in the crossfire, so to speak. She couldn't risk that. So she had that guy throw his paper your way, hoping you'd rent this room. And you did. Now that she's dead …' He paused and sniffled. 'N-now that she's gone, it turns out she was right about everything. About what you are. That's why I'm here. To fill you in on what you need to do.'

'And what is it then? That I need to do?' I almost didn't want to know the answer.

'You already know. You need to catch her killer. For a short while, I shall be your familiar. But you're *not* my witch. Maureen was. I'm only here with you to help you find the beast who killed her. She suspected it would be that way, just like it was with Wanda. It's only the first of the Wayfarer's talents you've inherited, and it won't be the last. But it might be the most helpful talent of all. If Maureen was right – which clearly she was – then you'll have the familiars of a whole lot of murdered witches come to you over the course of your life. They'll stay with you for a short time, help you find whoever killed their witch. And then they'll leave you.'

My head was beginning to hurt. This was all too much to take in. 'But then … why are you the only familiar who's come to me? Maureen wasn't the only murder victim.'

He held out his paw and I handed him yet another tiny bar of soap. 'Don't ask me. Maureen was the expert. Maybe because all the murders are connected you only get one witness?'

Fine, I thought, but did it have to be the smelliest one? 'And were you? A witness? Did you actually see who killed her?'

'No.' He hung his little ratty head. For a moment, I almost found him adorable. 'But it wouldn't have been much help if I did, would it? The murderers aren't really the murderers are they? I mean, you have figured out that much at least?'

I cleared my throat. I no longer found him adorable. If anything, he was a smart-arse. 'Of course. Of course I have.' It was true. I *had.* I'd just temporarily forgotten. Not dumb. Just ditzy. 'I just meant, you know … did you see anyone over the last few days that you and Maureen thought could be behind it all?'

'No one. Can I have my towel, please?' He held out his arms. Or his front legs. You know what I mean. 'But I *am* going to help you find out who it was. Because the sooner we catch whoever killed my witch, the sooner I can die and be with her again.'

9.Privileged

Dudley and I didn't go to sleep after his bath. We spent the entire night talking, instead. Of all the slumber parties I've had, it was by far the strangest. And after getting no sleep whatsoever, the last thing I needed was to be up at the crack of dawn. But I wasn't going to let a little exhaustion stop me. When I told my mother I was staying here, I hadn't told her the whole reason why. Yes, I thought it would be unfair to leave Max stuck finding another housemate. But it would be even *more* unfair to leave him unpunished for yesterday's trick.

I sat, bleary-eyed, on a chair close to the back door. Right on cue, just as the sun was rising, the door opened, and an enormous, shaggy mutt sauntered in.

'Good morning,' I said sweetly. 'Nice to see you again.'

The dog skittered to a stop and stared at me. 'Oh. You're up early. Again.'

'Well, of course I am. Seemed like the only chance I was going to get to speak with you. Seeing as you're such an early riser yourself.'

'Oh. Brilliant.' The dog's eyes took on a slightly pained look. They were changing before my gaze. Whites around the edges, where once they'd been all brown. The legs seemed to be growing longer, too. 'What did you … what did you want to talk to me about?'

'Well everything, of course.' I shot him my most winning smile. 'I mean, that's what witches do with their familiars, isn't it? Share secrets and gossip all day long? And my period's due in a couple of days, so I'd *really* love to curl up under a blanket and have a good gossip. I get the worst cramps, you know, and even worse pre-menstrual stress, so I *really* need someone to talk to about it. Maybe we could share a jumbo bar of chocolate while we're at it. Oh, but I'm on my way to work now, so you'll have to come with me so we can chat in the meantime. I could get you a lead and collar along the way. Or I could accessorize you, if you liked – you know, have you charmed into a piece of jewellery so you can go *everywhere* with me. I saw a witch at the Hilltop Hotel who wears her cat as a brooch. It's sooooo lush.'

'Em … well … I … that sounds lovely. B-but I have to go to the d-dentist this morning. The doggie dentist. Yes. And then …'

I let him stutter out a few more excuses, wondering how long he would last. His paws were changing as I watched. His toes were growing fatter and less hairy. His tail was shrinking, too. How long more could I let him suffer?

'Oh, just go ahead and change, Max.'

His eyes widened. Whether I'd told him to change or not hardly mattered, because it was happening in front of my eyes. Before I knew it, my new housemate was standing tall in front of me. His hands went to cover up his manhood – thankfully, I'd averted my eyes in anticipation, and had seen nothing at all – while his face turned puce. I pulled a bathrobe out from behind my chair and tossed it his way.

'You're a weredog,' I said while he pulled the robe on.

'I am.' His face was still bright red. 'But I mean … I assumed you *knew* when you moved in. But then you acted like you hadn't got a clue that Westerly was an *other* enclave. And then when I saw you so scared to find me in the kitchen yesterday morning, I panicked. I said the first thing that sprang to my mind. It's kind of funny. When you think about it.'

I narrowed my eyes. 'Hilarious. Seeing as I'm Wanda Wayfair. Unempowered. The witch with no magic and no familiar. What a *funny* joke, Max. Make poor, powerless Wanda believe she *might* just have some power after all. Because if she has a familiar, then she *must* be coming into her magic, right? That's not a cruel trick at all. Right?'

His eyes rounded. 'N-No! I mean … I didn't mean it that way. You were terrified when you heard me speak. And then I remembered something I'd heard about you. That you didn't spend any time in the supernatural enclaves. So I figured I'd scared the life out of you and I'd better calm you down. That's all it was. That's all I meant. I wasn't teasing you about not having magic, Wanda. Believe me. I mean, let's face it. Weredogs are hardly in a position to make fun of witches, now are they? Even unempowered ones.'

I kept a scowl in place. He seemed genuine enough, I supposed. But the truth was I didn't know much about weredogs at all. I knew that they changed into dogs for three nights out of every month, when the moon was full. And I knew that, despite all evidence to the contrary, they were absolutely and in no way related to werewolves. Both the werewolves and the weredogs were *very* insistent on that point.

'Well.' I stood up, taking my keys and bag from the kitchen table. 'I have to get off to work now. I suppose we can talk more later. Your cousin? Is she one too?'

He nodded. 'She's still away, though. Look, the full moon is over for this month, so I can finally give you a proper welcome to the house, if you like. I'll take you out for dinner. Or order in. Whichever you prefer.'

'Maybe.' I turned for the door. 'Oh, and by the way, there's a rat in my room. He's supposed to be here. He's my pet. So try not to eat him.'

≈

During our talk the night before, Dudley and I had agreed that my mother was probably right. Acting like I was still unempowered was a good idea. It would make people lower their defences around me. So with that in mind, I was leaving him behind for the day. And I was also, for the first time in quite a while, wearing my Pendant of Privilege.

I wasn't a particularly sexy dresser. I kept my shirts buttoned fairly high, and I rarely wore low-cut tops. Not because I was shy. It was a throwback to my earlier years. On the occasions when I *had* to wear my Pendant of Privilege as a child, I did my very best to hide it. Most people knew I was unempowered, but at least I wasn't giving them a great big shiny reminder. Even though I rarely wore it these days, the old habit of high necks had been a hard one to break.

Today, though, I was wearing my pendant loud and proud. And, if you've ever seen a Pendant of Privilege, you'll know that I mean it when I describe it as loud. Loud, garish, tacky … take your pick. Whoever designed these things did *not* want the unempowered to blend into the crowd.

The chain was long and thick, and always put me in mind of paperclips – except that it was a bright, yellowish gold. The pendant itself was round, made of the same yellowish gold with an enormous green stone at its centre. Not a pretty emerald shade of green. Not the colour of jade, nor of fresh green grass. No. Because any of those would have been far too nice for the likes of the unempowered (Do I sound bitter? I need to watch that.). *This* green was the colour of snot. Literally. The dark green snot of a bad infection.

So today I matched my oh-so-subtle pendant with a low-cut blouse that *was* a nice shade of minty green. I teamed both with a knee-length black skirt and a pair of pretty but not-too-teetery (all words had to get invented sometime, right?) black shoes. I looked almost presentable.

You know, as long as you ignored the monstrosity hanging around my neck.

When I turned the company van into the carpark at Berrys' Bottlers, I hoped to be the first one to arrive. Unfortunately, it seemed like the rest of the work force had an unhealthy attitude towards their job – everyone else was early too.

Grumbling beneath my breath, I made my way inside. There were people everywhere. I'd never be able to grab a bottle unnoticed. So I clumped up the stairs to what I'd been told was the accounting office, and hoped I'd get a chance later on.

'Ah, Wanda.' A short, bald, rotund man fixed me with a friendly grin and outstretched his hand. 'I'm Mike. Senior accountant for the Berrys. You'll be working with me today.' He nodded to a mini fridge next to the door. 'Plenty of drinks in there if you're thirsty.' He took out a bottle of Berry Good Go juice and held it up. 'Would you like one? It's hot today, isn't it?'

Well, that was easier than I thought. I grabbed the bottle and thanked him, trying to hide my relief.

Mike seemed lovely, to say the least. He was definitely approaching retirement age, and he had the rings beneath his eyes to prove that he was *more* than ready to say goodbye to the work life. But despite his tiredness, he was a patient teacher, showing me everything I needed to know about their accounts.

'Your final exam's this Friday?' he asked when we'd gotten to the end of the wage run, and the printer was finally chugging out the wage slips.

'It is. I'll finally be fully qualified.'

'Well …' He moved his chair closer to mine. '… once you are, I have a cousin who's looking for an accountant. It's in the office of a sewage plant but … I mean, anywhere's got to be better than here.'

I blinked. 'Excuse me?'

'I shouldn't be saying this,' he whispered. 'But the Berrys will eat you alive, Wanda. I do *everything* for them. Not just here. The coven have more companies than they can count. Here *and* in the supernatural enclaves. And I have to do the accounts for every single one. Not only that, but the coven have me doing some *pretty* unsavoury things. To be honest, I'm surprised they're letting me retire in one piece, what with all the dirt I have on them.'

'I thought … I thought you were human.'

'I am,' he said, pulling out a chain from beneath his shirt. It was a pendant, just like mine. 'I wasn't sure if you knew what they were, but seeing as they've given you a pendant too, you must do. They're obviously preparing you to take over from me after I retire. And you seem like such a nice young girl, Wanda. You can do better. I mean, do you even know how difficult it is to get your head around *their* kinds of currency? Do you? And I'm not talking about those weird coins. I mean sure, they take some getting used to, but the other stuff? Have you heard of some of the ways they barter?'

I shook my head, swallowing. 'No. No, I can't say that I know about any of that.' That much was true. I'd left home before I had to deal with anything so practical in the witch world. I'd have to ask my mother about bartering systems later. Right now, I had more important questions for Mike. 'So they're shady, then? I was worried about that. But I *really* need this job and they're paying me well. If I'm going to leave the company, then I need a good reason. Specifics. Like … what's this dirt that you have on them?'

Just as he opened his mouth to reply, the office door swung open. I was about to shoot whoever it was an angry scowl. I mean, talk about picking your moments. But when I saw who had just come in, all I could do was form a great big dumb smile.

It seemed a little less dumb when I realised that Will was smiling just as dumbly back at me. After a moment, he laughed in embarrassment and approached the desk. Mike moved his seat back to his own workstation, and Will perched himself on the end of my desk, looking at me. Well, looking at a certain part of me, anyway.

He coughed. 'Oh my stars! I'm sorry, Wanda. I wasn't looking at your … y'know. Not that they're not … but …' His perfect face grew flustered. Sweat beaded on his forehead. 'What I'm *trying* to say is that I was looking at your pendant.' He reached into his pocket, pulled out a small velvet box and opened it. Inside was another pendant, just as ugly as my own. 'I was bringing you this in case you didn't have one of your own. I mean, I was sure you *would* but I've heard you never come to the witch enclaves if you can help it, so I didn't want to take any chances.'

Wow, I thought. Everyone sure did seem to *hear* an awful lot about me. Who were these people, I wondered, who were doing the talking?

'Not that everyone talks about you or anything,' he said, as though he read my mind. 'Just … y'know what people are like. Look, anyway. Never mind about people. What I wanted to ask you was if you'd come to mine. For dinner. Tonight.'

'To yours? For dinner? Tonight?'

'Yes.' He coughed again, closing the box and putting the pendant back in his pocket. 'I mean … I can barely boil an egg but I'll do my best. So will you? I mean, if you're busy we can do it another night. By it, I mean dinner. Obviously. It's just … there's something I *really* want to show you. Something special.'

Alarm bells probably should have been ringing. If the Berrys were as unsavoury as my mother and Mike suggested, then Will couldn't be much better. What if he was inviting me over for some underhanded reason? But then, what if I said no and missed the perfect opportunity to find out more? I mean, I could snoop around Will's house. Keep my eyes out for clues. And, you know, any other excuses that I needed to make to convince myself I *didn't* fancy the pants off Will.

'Yes,' I said with my most casual smile. 'That would be fine.'

Will beamed. 'Really? I mean … wow. Great. Wonderful. So shall I pick you up at seven or so?'

'You know where I am?'

He grinned. 'Westerly Crescent, right? I don't know what number, though.'

'Three,' I said, grinning back at him. Darn it. I wasn't just grinning. I was grinning like a deranged fool. And I'd been doing so well at playing cool up until then.

As soon as Will left the room, Mike glowered in my direction. 'So. You're close with Will.' Was it my imagination, or was there a touch of fear beneath Mike's glower?

I gulped. 'No. Not really. I just met him the other day.'

'Hmph!' He stood up, ripped the wage slips from the printer, and shoved them into my arms. 'Hand these out. I'm taking the afternoon off. And seeing as you won't be here on Friday, *I* won't be seeing you again. So I wish you all the best working for your wonderful new friends.'

10.Two Hundred and Forty

Berrys' Bottlers closed at five, but I couldn't go straight home. The place I needed to go to for Dudley's dentures was on Warren Lane, which meant driving into the city in rush hour traffic. Great fun. I would definitely have to practise travelling the way other witches did. You know, when I got over my fear of slicing myself in two.

I found the address in question, and looked up at the sign. *Little and Large Dentures. Helping you and your familiar grow old together since the Year of the Walrus.*

The shop was just closing, but luckily they had Dudley's dentures ready for collection. Maureen had paid for them ahead of time, but I saw another customer in there, handing over coins – some round and made of a thick gold, some sickle-shaped and made of a bright metal that I couldn't identify. Others were tiny, pretty silver stars. Those ones jogged a memory – paying for cream buns in

Caulfield's Cakes as a child. I shook my head, amazed that I'd actually forgotten about those beautiful coins.

I drove back to Westerly Crescent as quickly as my little feet could press the accelerator, pulled up at Number One, and ran in with the Berry Good Go Juice in my handbag. I'd managed to stash it there as soon as Mike wasn't looking. Not that he would have thought anything of my putting a bottle of juice in my bag, but you never knew, did you? He was hardly my greatest fan. What better way for him to deflect from all he had told me, than by making *me* look like a traitor?

My mother opened the door before I knocked and ushered me inside.

'Did you get it?'

I handed her the bottle. 'What now?'

'Ronnie's staying late at Crooked College this evening so she can test it. She's the Potions Professor there. We should know within a few hours. Do you want to come along when I go to meet her? It'll be good for you to get to know our contacts.'

I shook my head. 'Actually, Will Berry has invited me to his place. For dinner.'

'Oh?' My mother lifted a chestnut coloured eyebrow. 'Has he now? And do you think that's wise? I mean, we might not have tested this yet, but we all know what the results are going to prove. This juice is connected to the murders. Which means the *Berrys* are connected to the murders.'

'I know, I know. But don't you think that's even more of a reason for me to accept his invitation? Who knows what I might find out?'

'Spoken like a true Wayfair.' She sighed. 'Part of me wants to talk you out of it. Part of me is proud as punch. But be careful, Wanda.'

'I will.' I turned to leave, but paused half way. 'There's something I forgot to tell you before. There was a break-in at the bottling factory. Late last Sunday night. Will told me they couldn't find anything missing except for the Berry Good Go Juice recipe.'

Her face fell. 'Well that changes everything. If they had a break in …' She stopped speaking and groaned. 'If they had a break in,' she eventually continued, 'then who knows *who* is behind all of this? It might not be the Berrys after all.'

'Really?' I gave her a quick peck on the cheek, trying to hide the smile on my face. Will could be innocent after all? 'Even so, I'll be careful.'

≈

Max was sitting on the staircase when I entered. He had a scarf pulled up over the lower part of his face, covering his nose.

'Is your rat okay?' His voice was filled with muffled concern. 'Because he smells a bit … sick?'

'Oh. Yeah. He's just old, I think. He needs a lot of baths. Speaking of which, I think he's well overdue.' I cast an envious glance at the scarf Max wore. Why couldn't I have thought of that?

Max didn't move from the staircase. 'Oh, yeah. Well I won't keep you. Listen, did you pink about the pipe?'

'Pink about the pipe?'

He lifted the scarf. 'I said did you think about tonight?'

'Oh. About us having dinner tonight.' No, I admitted to myself. I hadn't thought about it. In fact, I'd totally forgotten he ever asked. 'I'm so sorry, Max. But it's my new boss. He's asked me to go over and work late. Maybe tomorrow?'

He hung his head. 'Lippen. I dow I was a baseball.'

Sensing my puzzlement, he lifted the scarf again. 'I said listen, I know I was an a-hole. Hardly the welcoming housemate. But I was really happy that someone finally agreed to move in here. I mean, it's not exactly the best deal is it?'

I wrinkled my nose. 'You said it was two hundred and forty.'

'I know.' He groaned. 'It's a *lot* of work to expect someone like you to do. I mean, you're a Wayfair. And you work for the Berrys now. But that's the way it is in the *other* enclaves. Two hundred and forty minutes of community maintenance every single month. You wouldn't see the werewolves accepting a deal like that. They only have to do one-twenty. And the vampires? That lot do sixty. They barely break a sweat. Not that they *do* sweat, but … you know what I mean. And they don't even do a decent job, either.'

My nose remained wrinkled. I recalled my coven looking at one another the night before and mouthing 'Money?' I thought back to all of the other strange comments I'd received regarding Westerly Crescent.

'Ohhh.' The truth was dawning. This must be one of the unusual barter systems Mike had referred to. I think I preferred the pretty coins. 'I don't have to *pay* to live here. I have to *work.*'

'You didn't know that?' He slapped a hand against his forehead. 'Well that'll explain why you agreed to take the room. I suppose you'll be leaving now. Pity.'

He finally stood from the staircase, slumping into the lounge. I really wanted to go upstairs, bathe Dudley, and then spend a ridiculous amount of time getting ready for my not-a-date. But Max looked so miserable, and apparently I was volunteering to be his company, because I followed him into the lounge.

It was a beautiful room. There was a large entertainment centre, a great view of the park, big comfy couches and walls lined with bookshelves. By the looks of things, someone who lived here read a lot. I wondered whether it was Max or his mysterious cousin.

I sank into a couch next to him. 'I dunno. Might be a shame to have to move all over again. What does this work entail, exactly?'

His eyes took on an eager glint. He reminded me of the dog he'd been that morning. 'So you're still up for living here? Really? Well, the work's not that bad, actually. We have to spend some of the time maintaining the witch enclave in Easterly Crescent, but they issue us with a temporary pendant when we have to do that.' He looked down at my jewellery. 'But I see you've already got that bit covered. And about a quarter of the minutes are for tidying up our own area. The wizards down the road will even let you borrow their gadgets for that if you want. Hedge clipping, road sweeping, grass cutting. Since that lot moved in, I haven't had to do much more than supervise the machines.'

'That all sounds fine. But just answer me one more thing.'

'Anything.' The eager look grew tenfold.

'Why *minutes?* Why not just say four hours of work? Surely that'd avoid any undue confusion?'

He shrugged. 'Suppose it would, wouldn't it?'

11.Lost and Found

Dudley's dentures fit perfectly. The lisp was gone, and he looked like a much younger rat. Still a smelly one, but younger was at least an improvement. Speaking of smelly, I was just drying Dudley off after an incredibly long bath when the doorbell rang.

'I'll get it,' Max called up the stairs.

A moment later I heard him pull open the door and, after some words I couldn't hear from whoever was outside, Max said, 'Come in. I'll tell her you're here.'

I glanced at my wristwatch. It was six forty-five. It couldn't be Will already, could it?

Footsteps rushed up the stairs and a sharp knock sounded on my bedroom door. I left Dudley to finish drying and went to answer.

'He's a bit overdressed for a night going over the books,' Max whispered. He sounded a little on the surly side. For some reason, that upset me. I decided that if we were going to live here in happy unwedded housemate bliss, perhaps lying wasn't the best way to go forward. Although I couldn't exactly be truthful, either, could I?

'Overdressed? Is he? Actually, Max … I might have been a little liberal with the truth earlier on. To be honest, I'm not sure we'll be working. He said he has something to show me at his place, and that he'll cook us dinner while we're there.'

'Oh.' Max arched a light brown brow. 'So it's more of a date, then.' The surly tone was unmistakable this time.

Hmm. Straddling the border between truth and lies was a little bit trickier than popular fiction had led me to believe. What could I tell him? *Well no, Max. It's not a date, actually, because he's a murder suspect and I'm going over there to snoop?*

'I don't know what it is,' I said, sounding a tad more exasperated than I'd intended. 'Does it matter?'

Max shrugged, turned on his heel and went towards his bedroom. 'Suppose not,' he said over his shoulder. 'Maybe I'll go out myself, then. Clubbing, maybe. It's either that or be stuck here alone with your stinking rat. Oh, and don't forget your keys, because I probably won't be here to let you back in if you do. Y'know – because of all the fun I'll be having.'

I was just about to remark that I was still using the spare keys and had none of my own *to* forget when he slammed his bedroom door behind him.

I scarpered back inside my own room. 'What was *that* about?'

I should have remembered that I was no longer talking to myself. I had a familiar now – however temporarily – and he was looking at me while he crawled into the little bed I'd made for him on top of a chair.

'You know perfectly well what that was about. Max hates the Berrys. Everyone does.'

'Oh.' I bit my lip, wondering why I was so surprised by Dudley's answer. What else had I expected him to say, after all? 'Well … he'll be thanking me soon then, won't he? Because the only thing I'll be doing at Will's house tonight is finding the evidence I need to prove that the Berrys are behind these murders. Incidentally … I was thinking of wearing that red dress.' I nodded to the dress I'd left hanging outside the wardrobe that morning. 'Do you think that'll look good? For snooping, I mean.'

Dudley rolled his eyes. 'I've been going through your clothes today, as it happens,' he informed me. 'Don't worry,' he added, noting the look of horror on my face. 'I doused myself with your perfume first. You might want to buy a new bottle by the way. But I think that the teal summer dress would look best. It's not as obvious as the red, but it'll still give a hint of cleavage.'

I gawped.

Dudley shrugged. 'I *meant* so you can keep Mr Berry's male mind too busy to wonder why you're really there.'

'Oh. Yeah.'

'And also …' Dudley lay back and opened his crossword book. '… I think you could do with taking a quick shower first.'

≈

Somehow, I managed to make it downstairs at only a minute after seven. Will was sitting awkwardly on one of the couches in the lounge, but as soon as I entered he stood up.

'Wow. I mean … you look … I mean … wow.'

I looked at the floor. I had to, because his sea-green eyes were looking particularly sea-greeny at that moment. If I looked into them for too long, who knew what would happen? My stars, how do secret agents *do* it? I was trying my very best not to be distracted by the short-sleeved polo shirt that brought out his biceps, really I was. And I was also doing my absolute and utter best not to breathe in the smell of his cologne. It was hard work, believe me.

'Sorry I kept you waiting.'

'Not at all. You're right on time. It was me who was rude enough to be early. So, um … how do you want to get there?'

I found a fascinating pattern on his plain white shirt to stare at. 'What do you mean?'

'Well … you're not … you can't … I mean, I have a car, but my aunt has a conniption when I drive it. Says it's unwitchly of me. And I have brooms, but I thought … you know … you might think I was being a bit forward, asking you to ride on the back of my broom.'

I tried to calm the flush that was forming – not just on my cheeks, but *every*where. There was probably some witch etiquette I didn't know about involving brooms. Maybe it wasn't a first-date sort of thing, riding on the back of someone's broom. It was just as well, I supposed. I mean, I'd probably have to hold on, wouldn't I? To his waist. I'd probably have to hold on very, very tight.

'So then I thought I could click my fingers,' Will went on. 'Or we could take the company van, because my aunt probably wouldn't mind if you were the one doing the driving. But that's not very gentlemanly is it? And you couldn't have a drink then, could you? So ... yeah. It's probably either clicking my fingers or walking, I'm afraid. Your choice.'

I followed his words carefully, doing my best to overlook the fact that his aunt's opinion meant *way* too much to him. I mean, had he even met the woman? Who in their right mind would give a toss what she thought about anything?

'We could walk,' I said. 'If it's not too far across the park.' And also, I avoided adding, if we walked I wouldn't have to hold his hand the way I'd have to if we travelled via his finger click. Because that would be almost as unbearably and illicitly delicious as wrapping my arms about his waist.

He bit his bottom lip and smiled. 'It's not far at all. A walk it is, then.'

≈

It was my first time walking through Luna Park. It was a beautiful evening, and there were dozens of people out. Now that I'd come into my power, it was easy to spot the different types of supernatural.

There were some vampires just coming out of their houses on the north side of the park. There was still a little evening sun, so they were well wrapped up while they mowed the grass and clipped the hedges.

There were some werewolves too. If I'd looked at them a few days' earlier, I might have thought that they were just some incredibly attractive young men and women, but now I could smell them. It wasn't that it was a canine smell. Well, there was a bit of that, but most of what I could smell was far more powerful. The werewolves gave off some sort of pheromones that I'd never noticed before. The scent made them even more attractive than their appearances alone might have done. One or two of them could *almost* give Will a run for his money. Some of them were tending to flower beds and scooping up rubbish, but others were standing at the edge of the park and … I averted my eyes.

'They're marking their territory,' said Will, noticing my shock. 'I'd forgotten about that, sorry. I don't walk through this part of the park very often.'

As we neared the east side of the park, I sensed the other witches immediately. It caused a slight burst of panic. If I could sense them, maybe they could sense me. A young female witch looked our way. She smiled at Will and he waved back. It seemed as though she was about to approach us, but her eyes went to my pendant, and she sneered and turned in the other direction.

I might be irritated later on, but right now I was just relieved. People didn't look past a Pendant of Privilege. If I was beneath even chatting to, I doubted they'd sense that I was now a fully empowered witch. But then another thought occurred. I'd had my power for a few days now. It had come before I ever realised, and no one seemed to have sensed it in *me.* I filed away a reminder in my mind: ask Mam if witches can sense one another's power.

There were other supernaturals on the east side of the park, too, all wearing Pendants of Privilege. There were a couple of werewolves and vampires, but mostly the supernaturals who were often classed as *other.* Weredogs, dayturners, wizards and the unempowered were emptying the bins and tending to the witches' part of the park. The witches played tennis or cricket, or sat around chatting in the evening sun, paying no attention to the people who were working around them.

'So … don't witches have to put in the same minutes as everyone else then?'

Will looked confused, then followed my eyes. 'Oh … you mean the community maintenance? No, we don't have to do any of that.'

I raised a brow. 'And you don't think that's a bit unfair?'

'Not really.' His confusion seemed to be intensifying. He genuinely had no idea why I was bothered. 'I mean, you didn't get to live in the human world for free, did you? You had to pay rent. This is just the same. Better, in fact.'

'Yeah. For you.'

'What? Look, I know you've spent a lot of time away from our enclaves, but you must know that unfair is the *last* thing it is. We give a lot to the other supernaturals. We put wards up around their enclaves so they can live in peace.

No, we don't clip the hedges or skim the leaves from the pond or whatever. But we don't *need* to. We could maintain this place with the simplest of spells if we wanted to.'

'So then why *don't* you? Why make everyone else clean up your side of the park if you could do it more easily with a spell?'

He sighed. 'This isn't going very well, is it? Look, I realise you've been living outside of our world for a long time, Wanda. But surely you knew how things were. Witches do so much for the other supernaturals. Things we don't have to do. You think those houses in Westerly Crescent built themselves? Because they didn't. Berry Materialization built them, as a matter of fact, under contract to the Wyrd Court. My coven's company built every single house in Luna Park. Two hundred and forty minutes a month is *not* a lot to ask in return. And let's face it, people don't *have* to live here if they don't want to. No one's twisting their arms. But we've made this community for them. We've made communities all over the world where supernaturals can live in peace. Is it so much to ask that they keep those communities looking their best?'

I rubbed my arms. The sun disappeared behind a cloud, and I was beginning to feel a chill. I thought back to the times I'd spent in Riddler's Cove as a child. Even back there, the other supernaturals had done all of the community maintenance. I'd just assumed it was their job, and thought little else about it.

'I suppose not,' I said, a little sulkily.

'Hey.' He stopped in front of me, rubbing my arms. 'You're freezing, Wanda. Do you mind if I do something to make you warm?'

My mouth went dry. 'Do what, exactly?'

He closed his eyes, mumbled some words, and heat shot out of his hands. I felt it course through me, making me feel like I was sitting in front of a roaring flame.

'Better now?'

I nodded. 'Much. And sorry. I'm new to all of this. The way you explained it made it sound a lot fairer than I thought.'

He smiled softly. His hands, I couldn't help but notice, were still on my arms. 'That's okay. And anyway, none of it applies to you. You don't need to put in *any* extra minutes outside of your job. You're one of us now, after all.'

The blood rushed from my body. Had he sensed my power as I'd feared he might? 'One of … of you?'

'Yeah. A Berry. Well, maybe not by name but … you work for us. There are perks. Didn't your housemate explain? Oh, well maybe he didn't know. After all, there've only been weredogs in that house before you, and none of them could *ever* get a job with us. But for those lucky enough to be employed by the Berrys, there are benefits, Wanda. A lot of them.' He smiled again. The spell was still working, but I was beginning to feel the sort of icy-cold that no fire in the world could melt. 'Now come on.' He grabbed my hand. 'We're almost there. You're going to *love* my surprise.'

≈

I'd thought the houses in Westerly Crescent were nice, but these ones in Easterly were on a whole different level. They were enormous in comparison to the house I shared with Max. And the house which Will led me to, at the very centre of the road, was the biggest of all. There was a long and winding gravel drive, lined with yew trees. Will rushed along the drive and, whilst I kept up with him, I felt as though I were dragging my feet. I kept thinking of the last words he'd spoken, over and over. Did he really see the weredogs as inferior to the Berrys? I didn't want to be the sort of girl who fell for an elitist jerk.

'Does the whole coven live here?' I asked as we approached the front door.

Will snorted. 'Thank the stars, no. We have a much bigger place in Riddler's Cove. Most of the coven commutes from there. This is just my folks' little city pad. My aunt lives at the end of the road. As for my parents, they're hardly even here these days. Mam's been in Tibet for the last few months. Dad's building apartment complexes in a few of the witch enclaves. He spends most of his time working. I have a feeling he'll move in to one of them once the building work is finished.'

The door opened in front of us with a creak. I half expected to find some towering butler behind it, but I guess Will must have used magic to open it, because there was no one in sight.

'Well,' he held out a hand. 'After you, my lady.'

Taking in a deep breath, I entered the hall. The ceiling was far above me, decorated with golden stars and moons. There was a chandelier in the centre, each of its jewels shining like the evening sun. I suddenly missed my own cosy coven home a great deal.

'Come on,' he said, 'the surprise is in my bedroom.'

I expect my face must have told him exactly what I thought about that, because he immediately said, 'No, it's not like that. I swear. Come see.'

He led me up the stairs and into a large room at the end of the landing. The wallpaper was painted a pale shade of blue with vertical white stripes. The covers on his four-poster bed were a mix of light and dark blue plaid. The furniture was heavy, dark wood, and there was a plaid patterned carpet underfoot. The room confused me. It was masculine, I supposed, but in a very old-fashioned way. It gave me absolutely no insight into Will's personality. There were no ornaments, and the paintings on the walls were even more old-fashioned than the furniture.

'I know.' Will grimaced. 'I like wooden floorboards and simple, comfy furniture. But Dad gave Aunt Alice free rein with the decoration. She's his favourite sister.'

I hid my grimace as best I could. I couldn't imagine Alice being anyone's favourite anything. The nicest thing in the room, by far, was an enormous marmalade cat, curled up on one of Will's pillows.

Will stroked the cat behind his ears, and he purred, jumped up and – after rubbing himself up against my legs in the most delicious of manners – he sauntered out of the room.

'That's Fred,' Will told me. 'My familiar. I think he likes you. He normally hisses at new people.'

'He's lovely. Most of the Wayfairs have cat familiars, too.'

Will laughed wryly. 'Would you believe, not all the Berrys even *have* familiars. Alice doesn't have one. Nor my father.'

'Probably just as well. I hear some familiars can be *very* demanding. So … if not to admire your décor, then just what *am* I here to see, Mr Berry?'

His cheeks grew slightly pink. 'Oh. Yes. Of course. It's in my broom cupboard. I'll show you now.'

He approached a set of double doors in the wall and drew them open. The room beyond was certainly a broom cupboard. It was filled, in fact, with brooms. They lined every wall, carefully positioned upon brackets. There must have been at least a hundred of the things, and each one gleamed. The handles were of different woods, lengths and thicknesses, and the heads were made of varying materials. Some looked incredibly modern and streamlined, but others made use of more natural looking twigs and reeds.

There was one broom, though, that wasn't sitting on a wall-bracket. It was lying upon a long velvet cushion, on a table in the centre of the room. He gave that broom an awestruck stare. I could completely understand why. This one gleamed in a whole different way to the others. I could feel magic coming off it in waves. And there was something about the taper of the wood, and the twigs that made up the head of the broom. It looked so aerodynamic.

I blinked, moving closer to it, feeling the most unusual sense of sadness. Something about this broom … it brought back a hundred childhood memories that I'd long thought locked away. Saturday mornings in my father's workshop. Afternoons spent watching him fly.

Will coughed lightly, making me jump. My hand had been on the head of the broom. I snapped it back. 'Sorry. I shouldn't have touched it.'

He shook his head, a grin on his face. 'That's exactly what you should do. Wanda, this is for you. It's your birthday present.'

I gawped at him. 'But … Will …'

He approached the table, picked up the broom with careful hands and placed it into my arms.

'Oh!' I gasped, feeling a warmth of recognition. It was like holding a long-lost friend.

'You feel it too, don't you?' He grinned. 'I knew it when I saw this broom. I knew it couldn't just be me. I mean, I have a hundred brooms that your dad's company made before he … before he died. I bought this one a couple of days ago. Got it off some weird guy in the tavern in Riddler's Cove. He told me he found it in some lost and found locker in a Nepalese hotel. I thought … it could be the one, couldn't it? I mean, no one ever found the broom, did they?'

'What do you know about my father's brooms? I mean, you're what … twenty-four? Twenty-five?'

'Twenty-four,' he supplied. 'And yeah, I was only a kid when he was declared dead after disappearing on the Everest climb. But I was obsessed with his brooms then, and I still am now. When I saw this one for sale, I knew it was special. And I want it to be yours.'

Despite every part of my body screaming against the action, I placed the broom back on its table. 'I can't accept this. It's too much. We barely know one another.'

He reached his hand to mine. 'Wanda, I know what you're thinking. That I'm coming on too strong. But trust me, it didn't cost a fortune. And I won't see you this Friday at work, what with your exam. I wanted to give you your birthday present now. Please, take it.'

'Well …' I hesitated. I'd only known him a few days, and already I felt far too involved. His dubious remarks in the park had set me on edge, but this was bringing me right back there. And I didn't want to *be* back there. I didn't want to be staring into his eyes the way I was doing. I didn't want my heart to be beating like a drugged-up drummer. 'Really, Will, it'd be wasted on me. I mean, I'd never be able to fly it, would I?'

Would I? Good Gretel, what a thought. Flying, like I'd always dreamt of. Flying, like my father had done. Flying, on a broom just like his.

Will sighed. 'I know how you feel about being unempowered, Wanda. I could see it in your eyes the first time we met. You pretend it doesn't bother you. You pretend you're happy living as a human. But really, you want to be a witch more than anything in the world.'

I felt my eyes begin to smart. 'Oh. So it was a pity-hire then, was it? A *let's give the unempowered girl a go* sort of hire?'

'No!' He looked pleadingly at me. 'Not at all. Wanda …' He bit his bottom lip. Why oh why did he have to look so lovely when he did it? Why did I want it to be *me* biting that lip, nibbling it, sucking on it …? 'Wanda there's something I need to tell you. But you have to promise me you won't repeat it. On your coven's grimoire, Wanda, you *have* to swear that you won't share what I'm about to tell you with another soul.'

I gulped. Swearing on your coven's grimoire was *not* a thing one did lightly. It meant swearing on their collective knowledge, power and history. It meant that, if you broke your promise, your coven could lose everything they held dear.

And what if he was about to tell me something juicy about the Berrys? Something that would help the Wayfairs bring them to justice? How could I possibly keep that to myself?

'That's a big ask, Will. Especially when I don't know what it is that you're about to tell me.'

'It's nothing bad, I swear. Well, it *is* bad to me. But not to anyone else. Oh look, *I* swear on the Berry grimoire that what I'm about to tell you isn't anything illegal or bad or … or anything like that. Okay? So now will you swear?'

I studied him carefully. Whatever he was about to tell me, it clearly meant a great deal to him. But he'd sworn it was nothing bad. Did I trust him? 'Fine,' I relented. 'I swear on the Wayfair grimoire that I won't share what you're about to tell me with another soul.'

Surprisingly, he didn't look relieved. He paced the room, occasionally stroking one of the brooms as if for comfort. In that moment, he reminded me a little of my father. Except that he was shaking like a leaf, whereas my father had never been a nervous man.

'Do you want to sit down?' I asked.

He nodded, and I did a very silly thing. I took his hand in mine, and led him to his bed. Sitting next to him, my hand still resting in his, I felt *far* too many fluttery feelings.

After a few minutes, he turned to face me. 'I'm like you, Wanda. Or I almost was. That's why I wanted to interview you. To get to know you. I recognised your surname on your CV and I knew, I had to give you a chance. When I met you ...well, I would have hired you on the spot once I actually met you. Even if you couldn't add single digits together.'

I felt heat creep along my skin and did my best to ignore it. 'I don't understand, Will. You're not unempowered.'

His hand tightened in mine. 'I was almost nineteen when I got my power. Before that, I never went to public witching schools. My dad had private tutors teach me and had them sign blood contracts to keep my secret. I learned wizardry from some of them. Practised how to use the elements or to channel from objects of unusual power. I got good enough after a few years to be able to fake having real magic. Then I finally came into my power, and I didn't have to fake it anymore.'

I brought my eyes to his. Oh dear, this was getting bad. Really, really bad. Any longer and I might do something even stupider than I already had.

'I wasn't as brave as you, Wanda. I hid what I was. I went along with my family's lies. So I just want you to know how much I admire you. You did what I never could have done. Made a life for yourself in the human world. Turned your back on your coven.'

'Yeah, well, that might not have been the most sensible move on my part, actually,' I admitted. 'My mother is wonderful. All of the Wayfairs are. I wasn't being *brave* Will. I was suffering from a massive case of sour grapes and stubbornness.'

He laughed hoarsely. 'See? There you go again, Wanda Wayfair. Being a hundred times more honest than I could ever be. Sometimes it seems like every word that comes out of your mouth makes me like you even more.' He winced. 'Aaand I just said that out loud, didn't I?' He pulled his hand from mine and stood up. 'Never mind. No more embarrassing words shall spew forth from my mouth for the rest of the night. Shall we go and get dinner before it burns to a crisp?'

≈

Will had made a casserole, and it wasn't entirely ruined. Parts of it were even quite nice – you just had to dig a bit to find them.

'What would you like to drink?' he asked. 'I've got everything, but I did get a very nice bottle of champagne especially for tonight.'

'That'd be nice. But I don't want to have a hangover, so maybe I'd better have a soft drink, too. Um, do you have any Berry Good Go Juice?'

I know, I know, my mother had sworn us against drinking it. But I'd been with Will for a couple of hours now, and the only thing I'd learned was his deepest, darkest secret. Fine, it was pretty big. But it wasn't what I needed to know. Having the juice in front of us might give me an excuse to ask some questions.

He poured me a glass of champagne and one of juice. I took a sip of the bubbly first, then pretended to drink some of the juice. The flower pot behind me would be getting a thorough watering tonight.

'This stuff is so good,' I said. 'Hey, did you have any luck finding out who stole the recipe?'

He groaned. 'Not as yet. My aunt says she has an idea who it might be, but it's not exactly the sort of evidence she can bring to the gardaí. We didn't actually even ring them ourselves in the first place. One of the human security guards did. Alice is wondering whether she should tell the Wyrd Court about the robbery, or whether it'll cause more trouble than it's worth. I mean, what's Mildred going to do? Start up a competing company? That'd be kind of obvious, even for her.'

'Mildred?'

'You know, that vampire politician. Oh yeah, maybe you *don't* know. Lucky you. I wish I could forget everything I knew about supernatural politics, I tell you that much. Aunt Alice said the place stunk of Mildred's blood after the theft, so …' He began to clear away the dinner dishes, and brought out warm chocolate cake and ice cream. 'Sorry, the cake isn't homemade. It's from Caulfield's Cakes in Riddler's Cove.'

I took a bite. 'Oh my stars!' I tried to maintain my manners, and to chew slowly, but I hadn't had anything from Caulfield's in years. Between the broom, the cake, and my renewed relationship with my coven, I was suddenly feeling very fond of the witching world. 'So … is the factory owned by your aunt, then?'

'Yes and no. My aunt owns it legally. It's in a human enclave, so it has to be done that way. But the whole coven are very much involved.'

I took another pretend sip of my juice and followed it with some more champagne. 'Do you guys have a lot of businesses in the human world, then?'

'No, actually. This is one of very few, but Alice wants us to open some more. Berry Good Go Juice is Alice's brainchild. Her recipe. Frankly, we were all surprised that she managed to come up with a drink that tastes so good. Usually, she's about as good as I am in the kitchen.'

'Oh?' I felt my eyebrows quirk. Was I looking a tad too interested in all of this, I wondered?

Will put his fork down. 'Actually, do you mind if we move the subject onto something more interesting than my aunt?' he said.

So yes, then, I *had* been too obvious.

'It's just … I did have an ulterior motive in getting you here this evening,' he went on. 'Other than the broom, I mean. Wanda … I was wondering …'

Oh dear me, my brain was beginning to buzz. No, it was all out ringing.

'Eye of newt!' cursed Will. 'That's the coven ringing. I have to get that.'

I blinked. The ringing had *not* been in my head. The ringing was coming from a large, black telephone on the far wall. Will stalked towards it, picked up the receiver and, less than a second later he placed it back on the cradle. His face was paler than usual. His sea-green eyes had lost their shine. 'Sorry, Wanda. I'm going to have to take you home. An emergency coven meeting has been called.'

'Oh.' I stood up. 'What's the emergency?'

He gave me a regretful sigh. 'I'd tell you if I could. Come on. We'll grab your broom and I'll take you home.'

12.Wyrd News Nightly

As it turned out, grasping Will's hand while he brought me home was more tense than it was enjoyable. Whatever that call had been about had set him on edge, but he wasn't saying why. There was no attempt at a goodbye kiss, just a curt, 'See you at work tomorrow,' before he clicked his fingers and disappeared.

With my birthday present in my hand, I entered the house. As soon as I was in the hallway, music hit my ears. It was loud, it was folksy, and it was coming from my bedroom.

I ran upstairs to find Dudley lying on his little makeshift bed, a remote control by his side. The music he was playing made me think of hippies with flowers in their hair. I always thought I would have suited the flower-power era but, much as I was enjoying his music, I took the remote and turned it down.

He didn't protest, just looked at me and said, 'That was me and Maureen's heyday, y'know. Late sixties, early seventies. We were involved in everything back then.

Taking down the Wyrd Court. Making flying potions legal.'

I sat in the edge of my bed, taking off my shoes and rubbing my feet. 'But last night you told me that the Wyrd Court is more powerful than ever. And that flying potions are only taken by rebellious teenagers and ageing hippies.'

He sat up against the cotton ball he was using as a pillow. 'I didn't say we *succeeded* in taking down the Wyrd Court, did I? And as far as flying potions go, anyone who isn't on the stuff is missing out.' He let out a whistle. 'Great stuff altogether, so it is. Did you come back early so you could give me a bath?'

'No. But I'll give you one anyway. And while I do, maybe you could tell me some more about Maureen.'

'I have been thinking about it, actually,' he called out while I went to fill the sink with warm water. 'Not just Maureen, but all of them. I told you Maureen was a court representative on behalf of the supernaturals referred to as *others*, right?'

I nodded. During our strange little slumber party, Dudley had explained all about the supernatural legal system. The Wyrd Court wasn't just a courthouse. It was the governing body for all supernaturals. Witches had been the only ones with government seats for most of the life of the Wyrd Court, but in recent years the vampires and werewolves had been given seats. Their representatives were issued with Pendants of Privilege, so that they could enter Warren Lane, where the Wyrd Court was situated.

'Well, Maureen always knew her appointment was just given to her to get her to shut up protesting. If the Wyrd

Court actually cared about *others,* they would have chosen an *other* to represent themselves. They wouldn't have just brought Maureen in – a witch – to speak on their behalf. She took the appointment anyway, hoping she might be able to shake things up from the inside. Except it didn't really work like that. She was called in once in a blue moon, whenever there was an issue concerning a weredog, dayturner, wizard or unempowered. And when she was there, she felt like the Wyrd Court never listened to what she said. Like she was there so that they could dot the i's and cross the t's. To make them look politically correct.'

I carried him over to the sink. 'It was good of her, though. To keep trying. The more I hear about Maureen, the more I think I would have liked her.'

He sniffed a little. 'Yeah. It was hard *not* to like Maureen. Anyway, I was thinking about what connected her to the other victims. The one she knew best was actually one of the victims who got away alive.'

I remembered the item in the Daily Dubliner. 'Like Adeline Albright? My coven told me she's a librarian at Crooked College, and a chronicler, too.'

Dudley nodded, beginning to soap himself up. 'That's who I mean, yes. She and Maureen got on really well. They could chat for hours about magical history, so they could. Adeline spends most of her life in the library, keeping the compendiums up to date. The Compendium of Supernatural Beings is a favourite job of hers. Making note of what's going on, year by year, in each supernatural faction. Well, this year she made some changes. She made entries for wizards, weredogs, dayturners and the unempowered.'

I'd read the older compendiums, back in my childhood. 'But we're always listed.'

'Yes. Under *Other*. This year, everyone once classed as *Other* is now listed in the main section. Right under *Major Supernatural Beings*.'

I gasped. 'That can't have gone down well.'

'It didn't. So I was hardly surprised to find out that the chronicler had been on the hit list. I *was* surprised that she managed to escape unscathed. The woman is quieter than a church mouse. But you know what they say – it's always the quiet ones you have to watch out for.'

'And the other victims? I mean, Melissa told me that Eoin, the guy who was killed across the road from my old house … he was a clerk at the Department of Magical Law. But Connor Cramer? Didn't he just run a candle shop?'

'Yeah. I'm kind of stumped when it comes to Connor Cramer, to be honest. But as for Eoin, I *definitely* remember Maureen talking about him. She said he was the best thing that had happened to the Wyrd Court for years. Said he was really going to make waves. He was in love with a human, and he was friends with weredogs and wizards. Changing things up wasn't just some rebellious whim for Eoin. It was personal.'

He was moving quickly through his ablutions, already on his third go-around with the scrubbing brush. No doubt he was as worried about all of this as I was. If we *couldn't* figure out who was behind Maureen's murder, he might never get to join her in the afterlife.

'It's only half past nine,' I said. 'What do you say we towel you off, and get over to my coven's house? We'll get to the bottom of this Dudley. I promise you.'

≈

As I wound my way through the weeds towards the house, the front door swung open. 'I'm in the kitchen, love,' Christine's voice called out. 'Come and join me.'

I walked through to the big, warm room. It was so good to be back here, especially after spending the evening in the Berry house. For all its grandeur, that place felt far from a home.

Christine was huddled over a cup of hot chocolate. She waggled her finger, and another one appeared on the table. 'Just one marshmallow, am I right?'

I nodded gratefully and picked up the mug.

'Melissa is upstairs studying her little heart out,' she said, passing me a plate of chocolate bourbons. 'She has her final exam on Friday.'

'She'll work with you guys then?' I questioned, slurping hot chocolate through my marshmallow, dignified as ever.

Christine ran a finger round the edge of her cup. 'That's what we're hoping. Oh, look.'

In front of the wood-burner, my mother appeared.

'Oh good, you're here.' She took a seat at the table, panting. 'I was worried about you. How did the snooping go?'

I nibbled on a biscuit and passed some to Dudley. 'I'll tell you all about it in a sec. First, what happened with the Berry Good Go Juice?'

She pulled the bottle from her pocket and placed it on the table, her lip curled. 'Well, we were right about *this* stuff. Ronnie ran it through as many potions' tests as she could think of, and there's no doubt about it. Berry Good Go Juice is an incredibly nuanced hypno-potion. It's been behind everything. A witch can drink as much of the stuff as they like, and it'll have no effect whatsoever. But as for a human … they'd be open to suggestion, to say the very least.'

'So … what now?' I wondered.

'I've filed a report with the Department of Magical Law,' my mother informed us. 'Told them everything we know, and applied for a warrant to investigate. The use of a hypno-potion makes it likely there's a witch behind it, so it's back in our jurisdiction. Once we get the warrant, we can go ahead and find the culprit.'

I felt a strange mixture of excitement and dread. All my life I'd wanted to be a fully-involved Wayfair. Fine, I'd done a pretty good job of hiding the fact, but nevertheless it was true. Helping my family track down a wayward witch was a dream come true.

But Will's behaviour at the end of our date had put me on edge. Sorry, did I say date? I meant business-like dinner together, obviously.

I quickly told them what had happened at his house. Going quickly had its benefits: it gave me an excuse to leave out one or two of the night's events. I'd tell them about the broom at some stage. It looked so much like one of my father's that I knew my mother would love to see it. But as for everything else that had happened? I mean, I'd held his hand for goodness sake. I still wasn't sure how I felt about that.

Dudley took the floor next. Well, he took the table, actually. He stood right in the centre of it, telling my mother and Christine all that he'd told me.

'So,' my mother said as she emptied another packet of bourbons onto the plate. 'What we have so far is this: Someone broke into Berrys' Bottlers. We know that they stole a recipe, but they could have done more whilst there. The Berrys *think* it was Mildred. That'll be Mildred Valentine,' she explained to me. 'She's a vampire politician. Running for presidency of the Irish vampire enclaves as we speak.'

'And,' said Dudley, 'she *hated* Maureen. She had an all-out row with her last year. She told her that as soon as she gets elected – because Mildred is *very* confident – that she'd do her best to make sure that weredogs, dayturners, wizards and the unempowered get chucked out of the supernatural world altogether. It'd be goodbye to Westerly Crescent, and any other enclaves like it.'

I crammed another biscuit into my mouth, thinking over the almost-argument with Will in the park earlier on. I'd thought his attitude was outmoded enough. But Mildred's? It didn't bear thinking about.

'Well,' said my mother, 'if she *did* break in to the factory, then she could have tampered with the Berry Good Go Juice while she was at it.'

Christine let out a frustrated little moan. 'And it explains the *ear* scratching, too. Fiddlesticks.'

'It does,' said Dudley with a nod. Then, seeing my confusion, he explained. 'Vampires can get in pretty much anywhere they want, Wanda. They can turn into a bat or, what probably happened in this case – they can turn into this sort of misty, vapoury stuff. They're nearly invisible when they do it, and they can get in through the smallest crack. Mildred could've vaporized herself, then whispered into the humans' ears and told them what to do while they were under the influence of the hypno-potion. Vampire whispers are ticklish, to say the least. Hence the scratching.'

'I have to admit, it makes a horrible sort of sense,' I said. 'But seeing as it most likely *was* Mildred, what will that mean for our warrant? *Your* warrant, I mean. Will we –you – still be able to investigate?'

Dudley shook his head. 'It'll go to the Peacemakers. They report directly to Justine Plimpton.'

'Oh.' My earlier surge of excitement was replaced with a disappointed swell.

'But we don't know it *is* Mildred,' said Christine. 'Not for sure. And if we mention it, we might never get our warrant. I think we ought to keep quiet, get our warrant, go ahead and investigate … and if we *do* find concrete evidence that it was Mildred, we'll turn it over to the Peacemakers.' She shuddered. 'And I kind of hope it was *anyone* other than Mildred. Because I've had it up to the back teeth with Peacemakers. I *hate* those guys.'

As Christine was speaking, my mother's pocket began to buzz. She pulled out her mobile. 'It's Ronnie,' she said, before answering.

The conversation was short, and one-sided. My mother slid her phone back into her pocket, stood up and said, 'Do you want the bad news or the worse news?'

There was a collective groan, and my mother continued. 'We're not the only ones who asked Ronnie to test the Berry Good Go Juice today. Justine Plimpton had her stay back and test a bottle a short while ago.'

'Well if that's the bad news,' said Dudley, 'then I fail to see what could be worse.'

'Let's get to the lounge,' my mother replied with a sigh. 'Ronnie says there's something on TV we need to see.'

≈

When I walked into the lounge, it looked the same as it always did, no matter where the house was situated. It was a large, comfy room filled with three old sofas, two beanbags, and a 1950s TV that still worked perfectly. On top of the TV's wooden frame there were half a dozen photos of our coven, a selection of candles, and a crystal ball.

My mother switched the TV on, and we all sat forward to watch. I had no idea what we were about to view, but I felt a surge of excitement. I'd never been able to watch the witch channels as a child. Well, I could watch them, but all I'd see was fuzz. You needed to be empowered to view them. Well, either that or you had to have one of the supernatural adapter chips, and TVs with those things installed cost a fortune.

In the top right of the picture, there was a banner that read: *Wyrd News Nightly, bringing you all the latest from all the enclaves.*

There was a tall, broad, mousey-haired woman speaking with a journalist. The banner below her told me she was Justine Plimpton, Minister for Magical Law.

'You must be relieved to have finally made an arrest, Minister Plimpton,' the journalist said. She was skinny, blonde, and looked about the same age as the minister – maybe forty or so – but it was always hard to tell with witches. The right glamour could make an eighty-year-old look thirty.

'More relieved than I can express, Sandra dear,' Justine replied. 'But deeply, deeply saddened to discover that each and every one of these murders was a Hate Crime. Three innocent people were killed – and many more attacked – because they supported the fringe members of our supernatural community. Both Maureen O'Mara and Eoin Reynolds campaigned tirelessly for the rights of those poor souls known as *others*. And they were murdered in cold blood because of their compassion.'

'And Connor Cramer, the candle-shop owner – what about him?' Sandra questioned. 'He was an *other* campaigner, too?'

Justine coughed slightly. 'Well … yes. In his own way, of course. He sold his candles in the human world, you see. Something that usually only wizards do. This raised some eyebrows, I don't mind telling you. But enough about Connor. Our Peacemakers made the arrest at eight minutes after nine this very night, so he and the other victims can finally rest in peace. Of course, something will have to be done about those poor dumb humans who've been wrongfully arrested already but … all in good time.'

Sandra nodded earnestly. 'Of course, of course. Those poor dumb humans. Can you explain to our viewers exactly how it was that the humans were wrongfully arrested in the first place?'

'That would be my pleasure, Sandra. This evening, it came to our attention that the Berry Good Go Juice bottling factory had been broken into recently. Once there, the burglar added a hypno-potion to the juice. Once ingested, this hypno-potion renders the feeble human mind even feebler than usual. Because of this, the *real* murderer was able to make these humans kill her victims with the merest suggestion. It's believed that she gave each of them a trigger word or object, and that once the humans heard this word or saw this object, they carried out the murder on her behalf. This is, by far, the most dastardly criminal we've arrested in quite some time.'

Sandra shook her head. 'Fascinating, Minister Plimpton. Absolutely fascinating. A hypno-potion of all things. Well, I can imagine your department will be working some heavy overtime hours to come up with a solution for how to extricate the humans from *this* pickle. There'll be some tough negotiating between you and the human authorities, no doubt. In the meantime, though … you've given us a few hints about the killer in question.

We now know it's a woman. So do you think you could give our channel an exclusive on exactly who it is that you've arrested tonight?'

The minister hesitated. Everything about her actions told me she was pausing purely for show. She was dying to reveal the murderer. After a moment, she said, 'All right then. But only because it's you. Hah!' Justine beamed at the camera. 'Just my little joke. I'm happy to share this information with you, Sandra, and with the whole of the supernatural world. Only by sharing, and coming together, can we overcome the sort of attitude which has led to these latest tragedies. So it is with the heaviest of hearts that I reveal the identity of the crazed criminal behind all of these murders. And that person is … Mildred Valentine.'

Sandra let out the sort of gasp that told me she'd already known. 'Mildred? Valentine?' She looked at the camera. 'Well, you heard it here first folks. Mildred Valentine, current favourite for presidency of the Irish vampire enclaves, has been arrested tonight for the murder of three people, and the attempted murder of many more. Tune in after the break for more exciting news.'

My mother switched off the TV and sighed. 'Well,' she said, standing up. 'I guess we know for sure now. Who's for a cup of tea?'

13.An Empire of Berrys

The next morning, I was just on my way out when Max arrived home. His shaggy hair was even shaggier than usual. His eyes had bags under them.

‘Morning,’ I said in my pleasantest of tones. Always best to be pleasant after a row, I find. It usually makes the other person feel a *lot* worse. Cruel, maybe. Fun, definitely.

‘Um … yeah,’ he replied, somewhat sheepishly. He was holding a carrier bag, and he nodded to it. ‘I got you a breakfast burrito. Mushrooms, beans, tofu scramble. It’s my fave. Thought it’d make up for me being such an idiot last night.’

‘Oh, were you an idiot last night? Gee, I didn’t notice.’ I checked my watch. ‘I don’t have time to stay and eat, but the burrito sounds great. Can I take it to go?’

He looked a little disappointed, but handed me the wrapped burrito and said, ‘Sure. Oh, I got you these, too.’ He pulled a bunch of keys from his pocket. There was a keyring with a big purple W holding them together. ‘I shouldn’t have left you using the spares all this time.’

Frankly, I'd long stopped caring whether my keys were spares or not, but the keyring was cute. 'Thanks. That's really sweet,' I said, heading out to the Berrys' Bottlers van. 'Oh,' I said, turning back briefly. 'I've still not met your cousin. Was it a holiday or a work thing you said she was away for?'

He looked at his feet. 'Um, yeah,' he replied, going into the house and closing the door behind him.

I had to stop seeing everything as a mystery. Maybe it was the Wayfair gene. But as far as mysteries went, Max's cousin was about the last on my list. Despite everything that had come out last night, I still wasn't convinced we'd found the culprit. For one thing, the Connor Cramer story wasn't really convincing enough. He sold some candles in the human world? Big deal. I refused to believe that was the reason behind his murder.

For another thing – and a much *bigger* thing at that – Dudley was still with me. Well, right now he was snoring and stinking out my bedroom, but you know what I mean. He hadn't passed on. He hadn't joined his witch in the afterlife. As far as I was concerned, that meant that her murder hadn't been solved.

So with all of that in mind, I wasn't ready to let go of my cover. I donned my Pendant of Privilege once again, and made my way to work.

≈

The factory was busier than ever when I arrived. I double-checked my watch, then checked my phone just to be sure. I was ten minutes early.

Alice teetered my way. She looked younger than she had before. Must've had a visit to the beauty salon, I guessed. Her hair was shiny and full, and her eyes were an even deeper green than Melissa's. I'd have to look into this whole glamour thing. After a couple of sleepless nights in a row, I needed *something* to make me look better. 'Thank goodness you're here. We've had to recall every single bottle of Berry Good Go Juice thanks to that harridan, Mildred. I expect you've heard the news.'

'I saw it on Wyrd News Nightly. Had to put my pendant on after I'd already taken it off for the night but it was worth it. We don't have a supernatural adapter thingy for our TV.'

'Oh dear.' She glanced at my pendant, her nose wrinkling. 'They really *should* do something about the design of those things. Anyway, we were lucky in one way. Most of the shops were already out of stock, so there aren't too many bottles in circulation. But we've had to throw out the batch that was *meant* to be delivered today and start all over. The staff all came in early to help out, bless their little human hearts. We had to tell them it was a quality control issue, of course. Could hardly tell them the truth, now could we?'

'Oh.' I glanced across at Will. He was speaking with some of the packing staff. He looked tired, and was wearing what he'd had on the night before. 'I would have come in earlier too, if I'd known this rush was on.'

Alice rolled her eyes. 'That's what *I* said. But Will wouldn't have it. He said you have an exam to study for. Well, I suppose he had a point. I mean, it's not like you've got any *real* talent, is it. Might as well gather all the human qualifications you can.'

There was simply nothing to *do* except gape. My mouth opened, and closed, and opened and closed …

'Well, let's get on with it, shall we?' She gave me a smile that went none of the way to her eyes. 'You can start loading boxes into the van.'

≈

They say that the working day goes quickly when you're busy. Well, *they* have never had to work with Alice Berry. Okay, work *with* may have been taking things a step too far. I was working *for* her, most definitely. I had to readjust her seat a dozen times that day. The air conditioning was never quite right for her, either.

When she wasn't complaining, she was reading magazines. Glamorous Witch seemed to be her favourite. I hazarded a guess that the magazine advised against sensible spectacles; Alice mainly squinted at the words, but every now and then she took a bejewelled magnifying glass from her purse and used that to get a better look.

At lunchtime we took a brief break – during which she told me I ought to watch my calorie intake because, after all, an unempowered witch like me couldn't trim my waistline with glamours, now could I? And after she hit me with that confidence-inspiring comment, she asked me to rub her feet.

I was beginning to wonder why the hell I was still here. I could pay my rent in Westerly Crescent with a few hours' work in the park, couldn't I? (Maybe Will had a point – the terms weren't so bad, after all.) And once I passed my exam on Friday I could always get another job. Okay, *if* I passed my exam on Friday. Because, let's face it, study hadn't been high on my list of priorities of late.

Our final task of the day was to put up a sign on the latest Berry acquisition, a little shop on Grafton Street. The street was closed to vehicles at that time of the day, so we had to park quite the distance away and carry the new sign to the shop. Okay, *I* had to park and carry the sign to the shop, along with a drill and a stepladder and a box of screws. Alice was somewhere behind me, talking and giggling on her mobile phone. To her mysterious man in black, no doubt.

When I reached the address she'd given me, I blinked. I was still blinking when she finally caught me up.

'Well? Are you going to stand there gawping or get the sign up? Just because you're dating my nephew doesn't mean you can slack off, y'know.'

I erected the stepladder. 'Sorry,' I said. I wasn't sorry. I was angry enough to smack her across her incredibly glamorous face. Too angry, in fact, to even process the fact that she'd said "dating." I mean, *was* I dating Will? Did I want to, considering he and Alice shared a gene pool. 'I just hadn't expected it to be this shop, that's all.'

I got to work, screwing off the old *Cramer's Candles* sign.

'I know what you mean,' she said, sitting on the bottom rung of my stepladder and beginning to file her nails. 'Witches don't usually bother setting up too many businesses in the human world. But I've always had a certain fondness for humans. I want to expand the Berry empire, open up more and more businesses in human enclaves. I think most of the coven are coming around to my way of thinking. It'll be good for people like you, actually. I mean, seeing as Will wants you to join our coven, then we'll have to find something you aren't absolutely useless at and – let's face it – you won't be much good at running anything in the witch enclaves will you?'

For some reason, I was beginning to lose my balance, mentally as well as physically. I grabbed onto the shop window just in time to stop my body from falling. But as for my mind? She *had* just said what I thought she had, hadn't she? Will wanted me to join the *Berry* coven?

'Can you pass me the new sign, please? And the box of screws?'

Rolling her eyes, and mumbling, 'What would you do without me?' she put down the nail file and passed the items up. By the time I'd finished hanging the enormous *Berrys' Candles* sign and climbed back to the ground, I was feeling dizzier than ever.

'Eye of newt!' Alice cursed. 'What does *this* bozo want?'

She was glaring at a male garda, who was walking towards her with a large box in his arms. I'd seen him before. He was the one who thought it was a good idea to give the bottle of Berry Good Go Juice back to Maureen's killer in St Stephen's Green.

'Here.' The garda dumped the box into Alice's arms. 'We're finished with these. We never did find the tape for the day of the murder, but I don't suppose it matters, seeing as *your lot* are looking after it now.'

With those eloquent words, he turned on his heels and walked away.

Alice threw the box to the ground, wiping her hands. 'Hey!' she screamed after him. 'The shop is under new management. Give this rubbish to one of Cramer's family, because *I* don't want it.'

The garda kept walking. The fact that he seemed to know about witches – his referring to *your lot* had been my big giveaway moment there – wasn't as surprising as it might have been a few days earlier. Clearly, the negotiations between the human authorities and the supernaturals had already begun, if the gardaí were no longer investigating Connor's murder.

I looked at the box. It was just your average cardboard packing box. It had 'Security Tapes,' written on it in black permanent marker.

'This day just gets better and better,' Alice said. 'I'm going for a drink. You can make your way back by yourself, can't you? And get rid of that rubbish while you're at it.' She snapped her fingers, and disappeared.

14.Lassie Come Home

Dudley sat propped against some cushions, munching popcorn while I searched the entertainment centre. 'There's a DVD player,' I said. 'But no VCR.'

'Do your coven have one?'

'Afraid not.' There had been one, long ago. But as far as I recalled some candle wax got spilled on it during a séance. 'Can you even *buy* video players anymore? I'll have a look online.'

I was picking up my phone to check the internet when Dudley cleared his throat and said, 'There's a player in Max's room. What? I was bored all day. He has *everything* in there, Wanda. Old records like the ones me and Maureen used to listen to. Old movies. He has it all.'

'Yeah. But that was all his dad's. He said he doesn't even use any of that stuff himself. I don't think he'd like it if *we* used it.'

'Oh.' Dudley gnawed at a piece of popcorn and spat the kernel back into the bowl. Charming. 'Is his dad dead or something?'

I shrugged. 'I dunno. And seeing as my dad is the last thing I'd like to discuss with Max, I'm not going to ask him about his. But we can't just go through his stuff without asking him. Do you know where he is now?'

'Work. At the kennels.'

'See? I don't even know where he works.' I scrolled through the numbers on my phone. 'And I didn't even save his phone number. All along I thought he was being the rude one, but I guess I've been just as bad. Wait – did you say he works at the kennels?'

Dudley nodded. 'And that's not at *all* humorous, Wanda, so don't go there. Look, you're going to have to go up to his room and get it. I mean, if you *ask* him for a video player you'll have to explain why. And this is a murder investigation, Wanda. Not something we can just discuss willy nilly with housemates whose phone numbers we don't even know.'

I was on the fence, I had to say. I didn't want to destroy what little trust I was building with Max. We'd already had that weirdness last night over my not-a-date with Will. But Dudley was right: this *was* a murder investigation. I was nowhere near a decision when I heard a key in the door.

'Are you home?' Max called out.

'Yeah, I'm in the lounge.'

He came in, a large pizza box in his arms and a bottle of wine in a carrier bag. His eyes went to the box at my feet. 'Videos?'

I clutched the box to my chest. 'Um … yes?'

'I have a player upstairs. And I brought pizza and wine. Maybe we could watch one of them together? Y'know, if you're not busy.'

Dudley was shaking his head. He was right, most likely. We couldn't share what we were doing with just anyone. But Max seemed so *nice.* Okay, at first he'd seemed incredibly rude, and since then he'd been a little on the weird side. But still.

'Max, when a witch wants another witch to keep a secret, they make them swear on their coven's grimoire. Do weredogs have anything like that? Anything that makes a secret un-spillable?'

'You mean like the Bone of the Ages?'

I blinked. 'The what of the what?'

'Our family bone. We swear on it. I mean, my lot don't actually *have* a family bone. Well, we did but … look, let's just say someone buried it a long time ago and they've temporarily forgotten where. Anyway. Are you saying that if I swear on the Bone of the Ages, you'll let me watch those videos with you? Wow, they must be good.'

Dudley spat out another kernel. This time he wasn't being disgusting. Well, not entirely. This time, he spat the kernel out because he was laughing. He clapped a paw over his mouth to make himself stop. But I really didn't think he could contain himself for long.

'Fine,' I said, doing my best to hold my own laughter back. 'Swear then. On the bone. Swear that you won't tell a soul what I'm about to tell you and show you.'

'Fine. I swear on the Bone of the Ages that whatever you're about to show me and tell me will not leave this room. Okay?'

'Okay.' I felt oddly relieved to be sharing the secret with Max. Yet another indication that maybe I wasn't cut out for the spy-life. 'These are the security tapes from Cramer's Candles. You can watch them with me.'

'For the love of dogs!' he exclaimed, his brown eyes lighting up. He tossed the pizza and wine onto the coffee table and ran upstairs. A moment later he thundered back down, a dusty video player in his arms.

'We have to stick them on,' he said. 'Now.'

As he began to fiddle with wires and … other wires (I'm well-versed in technical things, as you can tell) I carried the box of tapes over. 'Max, do you know something about all of this? Because if you do, you need to tell me.'

His eyes began to water. Good Gretel, he was as bad at keeping things to himself as I was. 'No. Yes. Look, last night the murderer was apparently caught, right?'

'Right.'

He shook his head. 'Wrong. I hate Mildred Valentine. She's always been out to get weredogs. If anyone wants to see that woman locked away, it's me. But Wanda, I *know* she can't be the murderer. Because if she was, then Lassie would have come home.'

Oh dear. This time, Dudley could *not* hold it in.

≈

You might think that twenty-three security tapes – each one featuring eight hours of footage from a small candle store on Grafton Street – would make for incredibly interesting viewing. You would be wrong.

Luckily, we had popcorn, pizza and wine.

'This pizza's nice,' I said, reaching for my third slice. 'The cheese is weird. Tasty, but weird.'

'It's vegan,' Max mumbled, fast forwarding through a scene that featured Connor Cramer rearranging one of his shelves. It was riveting. I would have liked to watch it in full myself. 'And don't laugh. I think you and your rat have laughed quite enough at my expense for one day. Yes, I'm a vegan weredog. Big deal. Lots of us are. I mean, if you had to spend three nights of every month eating whatever you found in restaurant bins, you'd soon go vegan too.'

'Wayfairs don't go in for a lot of meat either,' I told him. 'In the old days, they had to break up a *lot* of sacrifices. There's only so much burning flesh you can encounter before you go off meat for good. Wait. Rewind that bit. Press play again from where the shop door opens.'

Max rewound the video to the correct point. As he pressed play again, his face grew pale. He was staring at the screen, even more transfixed than I was.

A young woman had entered the shop. She had long, shaggy brown hair and big brown eyes. She sidled towards Connor Cramer, pinched his behind, and grinned. Connor turned towards her, gathered her in his arms and … well … let's just say they showed each other a *lot* of affection. And, as it turns out, when you fast forward through such moments, you still see quite a bit more than you might care for.

'You know her?' Dudley asked gently.

Max nodded. 'That's Lassie. My cousin. And I haven't seen her for days.'

Dudley and I exchanged glances. For once, we were both mature enough to understand when a situation merited a calm, caring demeanour instead of riotous laughter.

'Tell us about her,' I said gently. 'Tell us what you know.'

Max refilled our glasses, and began.

'Lassie met Connor last summer. They fell madly, deeply in love. But they couldn't meet up here, or in the witch enclave, so Connor rented a little flat in Rathmines. They were talking about coming out. They'd even been to speak to Eoin Reynolds about it. He was talking about campaigning for new legislation. The law says that weredogs can't intermarry with *anyone.* Eoin wanted to change that law.'

I gasped. 'You know he was another of the victims, right?'

Max sighed. 'I know he was. He was also my best friend. I've been devastated about Connor and Eoin, and I've not been able to say a word to anyone. Because weredogs and witches are *never* friends. I was even worried about you being here, unempowered or not. But then I realised you worked for the Berrys, so I figured you'd be all right. I mean, no one messes with the Berrys, do they?'

I took a sip of my wine. Tomorrow's exam was looking better than ever. And why did *everyone* think I was one of the Berrys now? I was their accounting assistant slash minion for goodness sake. 'You said you knew that Mildred couldn't be the murderer because if she was …' I coughed. '… if she was, then Lassie would have come home. Tell me, do you know where Lassie is?'

Max shook his head miserably. 'No idea. She rang me on the day it happened to tell me she was going on the run, but she hasn't phoned me since. She said … she said she saw who did it. She was in the back, behind the curtains. She always hid there when the bell rang in case anyone saw them together. The shop filled up pretty quick, because Connor had a sale on jasmine-scented tea lights that day, so … anyway, she said there was someone she recognised in the shop, and they were standing behind a human. She said they whispered "*Cluedo*" and then the human just went wild and bashed Connor with the candlestick, over and over and over …'

I patted his hand. He was shaking and crying. 'Max,' I said softly. 'The footage from the day of the murder is missing. The garda said so when he handed these boxes to Alice Berry today. I'd hoped to find something else on the tapes that would give me a clue but … I don't think I'm going to find anything better than Lassie. And I kind of already know the answer to this but … I don't suppose she gave you *any* idea of who she might have seen in the shop?'

'No. But she said that the person saw *her*. She said it was a powerful woman, and that the woman told her that if Lassie breathed a word of what she saw, she'd make sure that every single one of Lassie's family and friends would be put down. And I doubt she meant with the use of a nice sleepy-go-bye-bye-drug.'

15.The Water Bowl

I took a taxi to the exam hall. I'd stopped after two glasses of wine, so a hangover wasn't the issue. The issue was one that I *should* have given more consideration to on the days preceding the exam, rather than on the day itself. I hadn't studied. Not for days.

Despite my lack of preparation, the exam felt like it went all right – but then again, my judgement hadn't been stellar of late. As I was leaving the hall I turned on my phone, and a text message came through from Will:

Happy Birthday, Wanda. And good luck with your exam. I haven't been able to speak to you as much as I would've liked this last couple of days. Maybe I could meet you after the exam for a combined celebration/explanation.

Oh, bugger. I took in a deep breath and replied:

Have to meet up with family afterwards, but I'll get in touch with you as soon as I can. Would definitely love to see you soon.

Well, it wasn't a complete lie. I was very much hoping that I'd be meeting some family. Just not my own.

I made my way to Capel Street and looked for the side street Max had told me about. As with Westerly Crescent, once I knew it was there, I should be able to see it. Sure enough, I soon found a sign I'd never seen before: Eile Street.

I turned onto the street, wondering what to expect. Westerly Crescent was the only *other* enclave I'd encountered, though I'd always known they existed. As I took my first steps along Eile Street, though, I realised the set up was far different. The very first area was clearly for unempowered witches. The first store I passed was a bookshop, with titles in the front like *Spells for Dummies: Simple spells even the Unempowered can master* and *Finding the Power Within: The inspirational biography of an Unempowered witch.*

The shop next to that one sold crystals and charms, designed to increase power, and the rest of the stores went on in much the same vein. Across the street though, the shops were most definitely geared towards wizards. There were shops selling technical gadgets, as well as a large building called *Wentforth's College for Wizards.* I put my head down. Unknown to any of my family, I'd taken an online course with Wentforth's College. It had not gone well. I never did go in for the final exams. I knew by that stage I wasn't cut out for wizardry, so I hardly needed an embarrassing *fail* on my record to prove it.

There was a café beside the college, and Max was standing outside. He waved at me and I ran to join him.

'It's just down here,' he said, nodding towards a lane at the end of the street. The sign said *Madra Lane.*

We passed by a small cluster of dayturner-focused shops, selling pills and creams that promised to alleviate any discomfort that might arise should they venture out at night.

As we turned the corner onto Madra Lane, I felt dozens of weredogs staring my way. I was about as welcome here as … well, as a witch in a weredog enclave. I wore my Pendant of Privilege so they'd think I was unempowered, but I doubted it made much of a difference.

Max led me to a pub called the Water Bowl. A large, blond man was standing outside the door. He was dressed in a dark-coloured suit, and was sweating in the afternoon sun.

He wiped his forehead, glaring at the pendant around my neck.

'It's alright Goldie, she's with me,' Max said.

Goldie grunted. 'Plenty of pubs up her own part of the enclave, if she's thirsty.'

Max sidled closer to Goldie. 'Saw this guy in the Phoenix Park last Monday night. Looked a *lot* like you,' he whispered.

Goldie grimaced, stood aside, and let me enter.

We made it three feet inside before I asked, 'What was he doing in the park?'

Max came close to my ear and said quietly, 'Running with one of the she-wolves from the Lupin Lane pack.

Let's just say that we're not supposed to mix with them, and leave it at that.'

We walked to the bar and found two free stools. I was getting a little bit sick of hearing who wasn't supposed to mix with who, to be honest. The barmaid seemed to have been told to expect my arrival, because she didn't scowl when I asked for an orange juice. She was a pretty redhead with light blue eyes. As she handed Max his chocolate soymilk she mumbled, 'Rover's in the back.'

Carrying our drinks, we followed the barmaid to a room next to the toilets. She opened a door into a room that smelled a little like wet dog. To be fair it had been raining earlier that morning. A card game was taking place in the room, and the currency seemed to be tiny, gold bones. It certainly beat maintenance minutes.

A huge, red-haired man with a gold chain around his neck stood up, said, 'Take a break, fellas,' and left the table. He took a seat on a corner couch, and Max and I joined him.

'You're Wanda Wayfair,' he said, sniffing me – thankfully, he did it from a safe distance. 'I'm Rover.'

I extended a hand. He sniffed that, too. 'Why are you wearing that ugly thing?' He nodded to my pendant. 'You already have your power.'

Max gawped at me. Then his eyes narrowed. 'Well duh! Of course you do. Dudley's not your pet is he? He's your familiar.'

I gave a shrug that was somewhere between guilty and defiant. 'Well a few days ago you told me *you* were my familiar. So I'm not going to apologise. And to be fair,

Max – Dudley can *talk.* You kind of shoulda figured it out already.'

Rover let out a deep barking laugh and patted Max on the back. 'She's a Wayfair, Max. She'll have her reasons. And don't worry, Wanda – no one else smells power the way that I do. Your secret's safe. Now, I've had a scent about, as we discussed.'

'Rover's got the best nose of any weredog,' Max explained.

'Yeah.' I nodded. 'I kind of got that.'

Rover grinned. 'I like you, Wanda Wayfair. Our Max has done good.'

Max turned puce. 'It's not like that. She's just helping me find Lassie.'

Rover shrugged. 'Whatever you need to tell yourself. Anyway, I wish I had better news. But it's like Lassie's disappeared off the face of the earth, Max. I got her scent on Grafton Street, around the candle shop where that witch died. There's a lot of witch scent in the area, too, but that's to be expected. Then there's a whole lot of lavender and peppermint and then … nothing.'

Max's face fell. 'The lavender and peppermint are good for disguising our scent,' he explained to me. 'She might have done it so I wouldn't find her.'

'It's possible,' said Rover. 'But those smells don't normally throw *me* off. I'm telling you, it's like she just plain disappeared. And *we* might not be able to make a thing like that happen. But a witch certainly could. Either way, I'll keep my nose to the ground. As for the other thing … now I've had a chance to meet her, I think you might be right.'

'The other thing?' I glanced at Max. 'What other thing?'

Rover laughed again. He put me in mind of a pit bull owned by one of my old housemates. The dog was mostly white with brown ears, and he was the friendliest little guy in the world, right up until the night the house got broken in to. He tore that burglar apart. Yeah, I thought, looking at Rover – he'd be a great guy to have on your side, but you'd be a fool to make him an enemy.

He raised a brow at Max. 'You're asking for special favours for this girl of yours and you haven't even told her? Do you even know if she *wants* a collar?'

Max swallowed, looked at me and said, 'Yeah. I should've said. The thing is, I spoke to Rover about this earlier. Things are getting bad for weredogs. Vampires are coming down on us. Werewolves have never *stopped* coming down on us. I think we need to make friends with some witches. As in, openly make friends. Rover agrees.'

'But these things have to be started somewhere,' Rover cut in. 'And where better to start than with a Wayfair? As witches go, your coven is one of the least unpopular. I'm the big dog around here, and I'm extending a welcome. But Max is worried about you being safe in the area. So to make sure the other dogs don't mistake you for an enemy, I need to give you my seal of approval, so to speak. I've got you a collar. Now, technically, we don't *have* any private enclaves. We're not allowed to have them, just like the wizards, the dayturners and the unempowered. But … let's just say we *all* mark our territory here on Eile Street. So if you're here again – or anywhere like it – as long as you wear a collar, then the dogs will leave you be.'

My mouth hung open. 'Collar?' All sorts of images flashed through my mind. None were pleasant.

Rover let out another of his barking laughs, and pulled a ring from his pocket. It was black, and covered with silver studs. 'This is a collar. What, did you think I wanted to put something around your neck?'

I snorted, putting the ring on my finger. 'Well, you could have *tried.'*

'Oh, I like *you,* Wanda. I like you a lot.' He stopped laughing and turned back to Max. 'Wanda can come and go now, in any of our private places. You have my word.'

≈

We left the boys in the back room to their poker game. Apart from my rather fetching ring, I was worried that coming to see Rover had been a waste of time. We were no closer to finding Lassie, and as long as she was still out there, I was sure that the real murderer was, too.

Max looked just as dejected as I felt. We sat at the bar once more. 'I might get something to eat,' he said. 'They do a great black bean burrito here.'

'You really like burritos.'

'I really do.'

I glanced at my watch. It was lunch time. 'Why not?'

My brain never worked well when I was hungry, so food was a pretty good idea. And the burrito really was good. It was spicy, but not too spicy. I was almost finished when my eyes strayed to a newspaper on the counter next to me: The Daily Dubliner.

The food was bringing my brain back to life. The sight of the newspaper brought the *In Dublin's Scare City* article rushing to my mind. Except now, things that hadn't made sense suddenly *did.* Cogs were turning rapidly, and I frantically tapped Max on the arm, but my mouth was too full to get out what I wanted to say. I chewed furiously, impatient to finish. He needed to hear this. But just as I was nearly there, the barmaid turned on the TV.

It was a *lot* newer and flasher than the TV my coven owned, and it clearly had a supernatural adapter chip installed, because it was turned to one of the witches' channels, and the weredogs seemed to be able to view it with no problem at all.

Sandra the presenter was back again. This time she was standing outside a building that I guessed must be the Wyrd Court. I could spot the roof of the Hilltop Hotel a short distance away. A tall, thin, black-haired woman dressed in a glamorous black suit was being led towards a van by a group of Peacemakers.

I shivered as I looked at them. Their uniforms were grey and black, more like armour than anything, and they wore tight-fitting helmets, leaving only their eyes visible.

'And there we have it, folks,' said Sandra. 'Mildred Valentine's plea hearing is over, and boy was it exciting. She has entered a plea of *not guilty.* That's right, folks. Despite the mounting evidence against her, Mildred

Valentine is insisting she is innocent. Her trial will take place tonight.'

Sandra held a microphone up to a man. Like Mildred, he was dressed head to toe in black. I narrowed my eyes. I *knew* that man.

'Mr Valentine, I assume you support your wife in this plea of hers.'

Mr Valentine nodded vehemently. 'Call me Basil. And of course I support my wife's plea, Sandra. Even though the evidence strongly suggests otherwise, I *know* my wife is innocent.'

Sandra patted his arm. 'The evidence is certainly damning, Basil. Damning indeed. You'll have heard that Peacemakers discovered her fingerprints at Berrys' Bottlers, tying her to the break-in there. But did you know that the stolen Berry Good Go Juice recipe was found in her private office this very morning?'

Basil Valentine turned from the camera, sniffled a bit and said, 'Oh no. Oh for the love of Dracula, no! Not *more* proof.' He sniffled some more, looked back at the camera and said, 'Despite this irrefutable evidence, I will stand by my wife.'

I finally swallowed that last bite of burrito. 'Come on Max,' I said. 'We have to go. I think I've figured this out.'

16.The Longest Library

I tried again and again, but no one was answering. Melissa I could forgive. She had a final today, and for all I knew the exam was still going on. But my mother and Christine? They *never* ignored a phone call from me.

'Maybe they're busy preparing your birthday surprise,' Max suggested as we ran through the city.

'Eye of newt!' I cursed. 'You're probably right. There's usually a huge celebration when a witch gets her power. Couple that with my twenty-first and good Gretel, I can't even begin to picture what they might have up their sleeves. Are you *sure* you've no idea how to find the phone number?'

He shook his head. 'Sorry. I know how to get in touch with the weredogs' directory enquiries, but that's it. Is there no other witch you could ask?'

I thought through all of the witches I could call. Will Berry came to mind, but I shut that idea down immediately. When this was over his feelings towards me might be a tad on the mixed side, to say the least – and my feelings for him weren't all that clear cut, either. If I *did* ask him for help, I wasn't one hundred percent positive that he'd *give* it.

I should be able to help myself, and that was the most annoying thing of all. I'd spent so many years ignoring the things my coven tried to teach me – facts about the witching world, spells in case my power should come. I thought I'd never need to know, and boy oh boy was I sore about that fact. But now … now I *did* need to know. There was no time to waste, and a phone call would really speed things up. Of course, my knowing how to click my fingers and get myself there in less than a second would speed things up even *more*.

Finally, we grew close to Warren Lane. We paused, partly for breath and partly because I needed to work up some courage.

'Are you sure about this?' Max was clearly as worried about the plan as I was – particularly seeing as there wasn't much of a plan to begin with.

I took off my Pendant of Privilege, fought to keep my nerves under control, and placed it around his neck. 'You know how in horror movies, the worst thing that the group of attractive teenagers can do is say, "Let's split up"? Well, right now, we're the attractive teenagers. And we should *not* split up.'

'But once you walk into that enclave with no pendant on, everyone will know you've come in to your power. Your cover will be blown.'

I took in a deep breath. 'It had to come out sooner or later anyway. And it's not like I know a whole load of people there, is it? Maybe no one'll even see me.'

'You might not know many other witches, Wanda, but trust me – they know you. But let's ignore all of the ways this could go wrong. Are you ready?'

I replied with a terse little nod. Grasping Max's hand for courage, we turned together onto the street. He looked just as frightened as I had on Madra Lane, and I couldn't say I blamed him. A Pendant of Privilege might allow him to enter a witch enclave, but it didn't mean he was going to be welcome.

Sure enough, we were met by wary stares. I didn't know any of the witches who eyeballed us. But I made a promise to myself that if I ever *did* get to know them, none of them would be on my Winter Solstice card list. Well, unless I figured out how to send a hex along with said card.

'Anyone get the sudden smell of dog?' one young male witch said to his little group of friends.

My stars, how I wished I could turn them into frogs. I settled for glaring at them, hissing, 'Watch your back, kiddos. Weredogs can give a nasty bite. And I can give an even *nastier* one.'

They skedaddled, leaving Max to smile gratefully at me. We walked onwards, passing the few businesses I'd already visited, and journeying into unfamiliar territory. Warren Lane, I was discovering, wasn't really just a simple lane. It wound this way and that, with many smaller offshoots leading towards alleys and cul-de-sacs that were *definitely* part of the enclave. The witches zipping around on brooms and having conversations with their familiars kind of gave it away.

'Please tell me that's it,' Max said after an uncomfortable ten minutes or so. He nodded his head towards a huge building. It was cut from dark stone, and had towers and turrets that soared up into the clouds. The higher storeys seemed far wider than the ones below. I guessed that there was more than good engineering supporting the upper floors.

The longer I looked at it, the more excited I became. It was a hundred times better than I ever could have imagined.

When Melissa and I were kids together, before she got her power, we used to dream of going to Crooked College together, studying Magical Law and becoming the most fearsome Wayfairs the world had ever seen. It was said that you could enter Crooked College from witch enclaves in major cities all over the world. Melissa could have entered the college via the Dublin entrance today, and popped into Paris or London for lunch.

I wondered if every witch was as blown away by the magical world as I was, or if I only felt that way because I'd lived without magic in the human world for so long. I let out a wistful sigh, and Max and I entered the building. Although the front doors were wide open, the corridors were sparsely populated, and there was no one behind the front desk. There was a huge map of the building's innards on the wall next to the desk, though, so we studied it.

'"The Longest Library",' Max read. 'Could that be it?'

I let my eyes rove, but I could see no other library mentioned on the map. 'Must be. It looks like it's on the ground floor, but *waaay* at the back.'

We took off again, rushing along the corridors, past lecture halls and labs, study areas and a *very* nice-looking canteen.

'I've never *seen* a menu that size,' whispered Max.

He was right; the menu board took up one entire wall of the canteen. There must have been hundreds of options on there. There were a few small groups of students inside, gazing down at books or practicing spells. There were more students seated in little window alcoves, also cramming in as much as they could. We passed one closed exam hall, and saw that it was filled with dozens of students. The sign on the door said, 'Magical Law, Final Exam.'

'Good luck, Melissa,' I said quietly as we ran past.

Finally we came to the library. We walked in through open double doors, entering what was most definitely the longest room I had *ever* seen. There was a line of tables and chairs stretching further than the eye could see in the centre of the room. To either side, the library was separated into countless smaller alcoves. I could see signs for Potions, Materialization, Glamourization ... every subject you could think of, there was an alcove dedicated to it – I could even see alcoves dedicated to Romance, Fantasy and Science Fiction.

'What kind of fantasy could a witch *possibly* need to read?' Max wondered. 'Every witch enclave *I've* seen is a fantasy come true.'

'I wish I could tell you. You can't read witch literature if you're unempowered. Hey, maybe the fantasy books are about working in banks or supermarkets or something.'

Max tittered. 'Or riding on a bus instead of a broom. So where do we start looking?'

'No idea. I can't even see the other end of this place. And we don't even know if she's here.'

'If who is here?' A woman appeared right in front of us. She was tall and slim, with strawberry blonde hair. She looked maybe thirty or so. There was a pair of glasses on top of her head, and another on a chain around her neck.

Oh well, might as well come out with it. 'We're looking for Adeline Albright.'

'Oh.' She blinked, put on a pair of her glasses and peered at us. 'Are you students here? I don't recognise you.'

'No,' said Max. 'But it really is urgent. Is she here?'

She took off those glasses, switched them for the ones on her head and looked at Max once again. 'I *do* recognise you, actually. You look just like your cousin. Except, you know, that you're not a girl.'

'Oh.' I breathed out a sigh of relief. 'So we were right. *You're* Adeline Albright. And you know where Lassie is.'

She gave me a cautious smile, then walked towards a little alcove on the right side of the room. There were more desks in there, as well as a long, comfy couch and a coffee pot. The books that lined the shelves all seemed to relate to necromancy. One book was titled *Dead and Loving it: How one woman rediscovered the joys of married life long after her husband had passed.* I shuddered.

'Would you like a coffee?'

Max and I muttered, 'No thanks,' and Adeline went ahead and poured herself a drink.

'How did you know she was with me?' she asked, taking a huge gulp of black coffee. How did it not burn her throat?

'It was just a guess,' I told her. 'You were quoted in the paper as saying you had to go home and feed your dog. And seeing as you had connections to some of the other victims, I figured you might have known Connor – and therefore Lassie – as well.'

Adeline goggled at me. '*That's* how you figured it out? That's not a lot to go on.' She swapped her glasses once more. 'Ah.' Her lips curled into a smile. 'But you're a Wayfair, aren't you? You're the one Maureen O'Mara told me about. She said you'd have unusually good instincts.'

'Oh.' I reddened. 'Well, that's nice. But listen, we really need to speak with Lassie.'

'No. I can't allow that, I'm afraid. No one knows where I have her and it's safest that way. Until Mildred Valentine is behind bars, anyway.'

'You think *Mildred* is behind this?' I asked her.

She shrugged, taking another huge drink. She slurped, I noticed. It didn't look ladylike, but it *did* look satisfying. Note to self: must slurp more often.

'Well, it must be Mildred,' she said. 'I mean, I saw it on the news just a while ago. And it makes perfect sense that it would be her, given the people she's attacked. Mildred *hates* weredogs. And it had to be a vampire who whispered the trigger word to the hypno-potioned humans, because otherwise, they would have been seen.'

'Yeah, except that Lassie *did* see someone,' Max pointed out. 'Which is why she's in hiding. What did Lassie say when she saw that Mildred had been arrested?'

'Nothing,' Adeline replied. 'I mean, I don't see how she could even know about it yet. I don't have a television, so I only just found out today myself when I visited the canteen for lunch. They had Wyrd News Daily on the TV. I was going to tell Lassie when I got home this evening. But given the fact that you two are looking at me with such abject disdain in your eyes, I'm guessing that you *don't* believe it was Mildred.'

'No. No we don't,' I said. 'Mildred's been set up. And Lassie is *not* safe. If I figured out that you have her, then it's not long before other people do too. Look, I know that Lassie is afraid, and she's right to be. But she's the only witness to all of this. Think about it. If you were the murderer, would *you* be happy knowing she was still around?'

Adeline drained the last of her coffee, then took off her current pair of glasses, and began frantically scrubbing the lenses. Just when I was beginning to wonder how many nervous habits this woman might have, she said, 'But … Lassie said that this woman told her she and her family would be safe as long as she *didn't* say a word.'

I snorted. 'You must have read a lot of books in your time, given you spend most of your days in a library. So tell me – do the evil murderers usually keep their promises in witch fiction?'

She chewed on the chain attached to her glasses. 'Well no, but … what do you want with her exactly? Because she'll never testify. She's not just frightened for her own life. She's worried about Max, too.'

Max took a seat next to her. 'I know she is, and I appreciate it. Look, you said a minute ago that Maureen told you Wanda had good instincts. Well, right now Wanda's instincts are telling her that the only way Lassie will be safe is if she *does* testify. And seeing as the trial is tonight, we need to speak with her as soon as possible.'

Adeline slumped back into her seat. 'Lassie never told me who it was that she saw. You *really* don't think it's Mildred? I mean … are you *sure*?'

'We're sure,' Max said through clenched teeth. 'One hundred percent.'

Adeline let out a long, shaky breath, and stood up. 'I'll write down the coordinates so you can travel to see her. But I doubt you'll convince her to testify.'

I looked at the floorboards. They were really very nice. Polished, but showing of their age. Classy. 'Now, when you say *travel* … I suppose you mean by clicking my fingers? Because the thing is, you see … I only got my power very recently. I'm not even sure when precisely. But …'

Adeline chewed on her glasses-chain again. 'I've never had more than one passenger before. But I'll give it a try. Wanda, you take my hand. Max, you take Wanda's. But I should probably add a disclaimer here, y'know. Because if I splice you, there's no point in suing me. I am *not* well paid.'

Max swallowed, but took my hand. I grabbed onto Adeline's, and we left the library.

17.Happy Birthday

As soon as we arrived in Adeline's living room, I knew something was wrong. And it wasn't just because of the signs of recent struggle.

Max growled – a real, actual, dog-like growl – and glared around at the mess. Pages had been torn from books. There were bite-marks out of cushions. A pane had been smashed out of the window.

Adeline let out a little cry, rushing from room to room. The whole house was in the same state.

'Lassie's not home!' she cried out in panic. 'Where *is* she?'

While she and Max ran about, growing more and more alarmed, I stood still, looking around the room. Poor Adeline. It was clear that, before this mess, her home had been beautiful. The walls were lined with shelves – for books that were now, unfortunately, destroyed. Her couches and chairs looked like they'd been the loveliest, comfiest places to rest before their upholstery had been torn open.

'We need to find her,' said Max. 'I'm going to search for her scent.' He ran around the room, picking up cushions and sniffing along the floor. Was it my imagination, or was he suddenly looking a bit … shaggier?

After a few minutes, he and Adeline stopped rushing about and looked hopelessly at me. 'Where could she have gone?' Max asked. 'Do you think the murderer took her?'

'No. I don't think the murderer *took* her. Not exactly.' I kept eyeing the room. Instinct had led me here, and now instinct was telling me that I needed to stay. There was *something* that wasn't quite right. I looked around once more. Ah. There it was.

I gazed to a couch that was bathed in afternoon light. All around the room, feathers and fluff from Adeline's cushions were swirling. But just there, they were falling differently. They were falling *around* something, not onto something.

'Alice, I know you're here,' I said, trying to sound more confident than I felt. 'Reveal yourself. *And* the others.'

With a huffing noise, Alice appeared. She was standing in front of the couch, pointing a finger at three people: Lassie, Christine, and my mother.

'Well *done* love,' gushed my mam. 'How did you know? Oh – and happy birthday!'

Alice narrowed her eyes. 'You can save the birthday wishes for never. But do tell us, oh poor, pitiable, unempowered Wanda – however *did* you know we were here?'

I ignored Alice and focused on the threesome on the couch. Max and Adeline were taking it in turns to try and get to them, but each time they fell back. There was an invisible barrier surrounding the couch, and surrounding Alice, too. I might be able to *see* them all now, but that wasn't going to make freeing them any easier. 'I take it that whatever spell Alice has you under, you can't get out of it?'

My mother and Christine shook their heads. Poor Lassie simply *shook.* She was looking at Max, tears falling down her face.

'It's an Insitu spell,' said my mother. 'I can usually break them. But it turns out that Alice Berry is more than just a glamorous face.'

'Of course,' added Christine, 'we didn't think we'd be able to break her Invisibility spell, either. But you managed it, Wanda.'

Alice wrinkled her nose. 'She didn't break the spell. *I* broke it. I decided to let Wanda see *exactly* what being a Wayfair can achieve.' She turned back to me. 'But I am impressed you managed to sense we were here. Impressed, but not surprised.' She pulled something from her pocket. It was the same jewelled magnifying glass she'd been reading her magazines with the other day. 'This,' she said, 'is an Aurameter. But if you'd bothered to learn anything about being a witch, you would have already known that. I had a feeling there was more to you than met the eye. *This* lets me see your power.'

'Oh yeah.' I ignored her again, speaking to my mother and Christine. 'I meant to ask you guys about that. I was worried that other witches might be able to sense me, and I meant to ask you if there was any way they could.'

My mother glanced at the Aurameter. 'There *are* witches who can simply sense another witch's power, but they're rare. Most witches do a Revelation spell to discover what they're up against power-wise. The Aurameter is something even a child could use.'

Alice clenched her teeth. 'Are all of you *actually* ignoring me? You haven't figured out just how serious this is yet, have you?' She turned to Max. 'This house is sealed. Sealed by a spell that none of these feeble witches could break. You're stuck. And you're all going to die in a tragic accident.' She turned her attention to me. 'I really didn't want to have to do this to you, Wanda. I was waiting for Adeline to get home so I could finish her and Lassie off together. But then your stupid coven had to get involved. And now *you.* Will isn't going to be happy that you're here.' She shrugged her shoulders. 'Oh well, once I tell him you're a double-crossing witch, he'll soon get over it.'

She moved away from the couch, mumbling an incantation beneath her breath. I couldn't make out the words, but I doubted I'd be able to do much about it even if I could.

'It's an Inferno spell,' my mother explained. 'And she's layering incantations so that it'll be on a timer. We'll be sealed here until she's well out of the way, then we'll all die. Oh, and just because we can't get *off* this couch … that doesn't mean that the Inferno spell can't get to us. This isn't the sort of barrier that keeps us safe, unfortunately. It's the sort that keeps us from running for our lives.'

'Oh.' I threw a cushion to the floor – well, the rest of the cushions were there, this one might as well join the party – and sat down in what was left of an armchair. 'That sounds like as good a way as any to celebrate my birthday. So why are you guys here anyway? You figured out Lassie was here in Adeline's house like me and Max did?'

Christine shook her head. 'No. We put a tracker on Alice. We suspected her all along. Despite the evidence.'

'We would have said.' My mother gave me a guilty little shrug. 'But we didn't want to worry you so close to your final exam. Oh, how did it go, anyway?'

'Good Gretel,' I groaned. 'Don't remind me. At this stage, all I can do is pray that the exam papers *also* get burned in an Inferno spell.'

Christine and my mother laughed. Adeline, Max and Lassie stared at us like we'd lost our minds.

'Have you all lost your minds?' asked Lassie.

My mother squeezed her hand. 'I can see why you'd think so, but we've still a few slices left in the old pan. I've just always found that my brain works better when I'm relaxed.'

Max took a seat on the arm of the chair next to me, while Adeline ran about the room, picking up what was left of her books, tears in her eyes.

'Sorry about the state of your hovel.' Alice shrugged in a most *un*-sorry manner. 'But the weredog put up quite the struggle.'

'Just out of curiosity, how did you know Lassie was here?' I asked.

Alice snorted. 'Really? You think *you* can figure that out but I can't? I always knew where she was. I intended to wait until Mildred was firmly behind bars before I came to kill her and Adeline. But when I realised you lot were sniffing around after me, I thought I'd better get it over with.' Alice looked at Lassie. 'Don't blame them, though. Like I said, I would have killed you in the end – all they did was force me to hurry things along. And as for our chronicler.' She scowled at Adeline. 'How *did* you manage to survive that attack? That human was ordered to stab you.'

Adeline cleared her throat. 'Well, perhaps you should have researched your victims a little better. I've been known to win a cage fight or two in my time.'

I couldn't say who was more surprised to hear *that.* But unfortunately, Alice looked like she was getting ready to leave, so questions would have to wait. And seeing as I still hadn't thought of a cunning plan of action, delay was the only option. Just as I was about to say something, though, Christine opened her mouth. Great minds, apparently. Or fools. Let's just go with great minds for now – I need the confidence boost.

'If you don't mind me asking,' she said to Alice. 'Why *did* you choose those particular victims? I mean, I know you're not all for weredog rights or anything, but I've never known you to hate their supporters *this* much.'

Alice shrugged. 'Well, you know, I hid my racism well.'

I snorted. 'Yeah, right. *I* know why you killed them. And I also know that you didn't do any of this on your own. There was a vampire involved in a lot of the attacks all right, but it wasn't Mildred. It was her husband, Basil. The pair of you set Mildred up. It's disappointing, really. I mean, of all the reasons to go on a murderous rampage, I think that "I did it for a man," has got to be one of the most pathetic reasons there is.'

While everyone else in the room gasped in shock, Alice glared at me. Her eyes seemed to get greener all the time. If I ever escaped from this, I might have to pay a visit to her salon. For a woman of indeterminate age, she really *did* look amazing.

'There is nothing pathetic about eternal love. But I wouldn't expect a snivelling spy like you to understand. I bugged the dining room the other night, did you know that? I heard you when you were eating dinner with Will, trying to get him to answer questions about me. You *used* my nephew. If I weren't already about to kill you for something else, I would *definitely* kill you for that.'

'You called the emergency meeting.' I narrowed my eyes. 'You did it to get him away from me.'

'Well, duh.' She placed her hands on her hips. Her eyes had taken on somewhat of a murderous glint. Well, more murderous. 'I told the whole coven we needed to discuss Will's possible relationship with a Wayfair. Poor, innocent Will didn't see the point. He said there was no way you were a spy. He said you were the most honest person he'd ever met. *I* said that if that was the case, then you'd consent to disowning the Wayfairs and joining the

Berrys. Will agreed that he'd ask you today. But guess what? When he asked you to meet him you turned him down, because you had more important things to do.' She came closer to me. 'Like betraying him and going after his favourite aunt. You'd *never* make it as a Berry. You have no idea what coven loyalty means.' She smirked, clicked her fingers and, just before she disappeared, said, 'But I suppose that doesn't matter anymore. You have five minutes, folks. Time to say your goodbyes.'

18.Inferno

As soon as Alice left the room, an enormous clock appeared, suspended in the air. Bright red digits shone against a black screen, counting down. We had four minutes and thirty seconds remaining.

'Well, that's dramatic,' said Max.

'It's good.' My mother gave the clock an appreciative nod. 'She's quite talented, isn't she?'

'Mm.' Christine murmured her agreement. 'It's a *beautiful* spell. More complicated than it looks. And do you know what else impressed me? She didn't overdo it, did she? I mean, yes, she went on a bit. But nothing like they usually do.'

My mother grabbed Christine's arm, a burst of laughter erupting. 'Do you remember …' She paused for breath, clearly finding *something* hilarious. 'Do you remember that witch in Galway? The one who was luring young female swimmers into her private pool and stealing their youth?'

'Oh my stars!' Christine laughed uproariously. 'I *do* remember her. We timed her, didn't we? A one hour monologue if I'm not mistaken.'

While they reminisced, Max, Adeline and I got to work. None of our phones were working, but hey, that would have made things too easy, right?

'The area around the clock is the epicentre of the spell, so to speak,' said Adeline. 'That's where the fire will come from. But the clock and the Inferno seem to have been interlinked, if I followed her incantation correctly. Break the clock, we *might* be able to break the spell.'

'I'll go first,' said Max.

'What, because you're the guy?'

He rolled his eyes, walked towards the timer and his body shot back across the room. Luckily, an upturned coffee table stopped his flight. He sat on the ground, rubbing his back. 'It's just like the couch. I can't get near it'

'Oh gee, really?'

He seemed to have a sixth sense for sarcasm, did Max. With a wide smile, he looked up at me, waved a hand in the direction of the timer and said, 'Well, little lady. It's all yours.'

I approached cautiously, feeling out the air. This whole magic thing was a bit of a rush, to be honest. Being able to feel power in the air … wow. As I drew closer to the clock, the air grew thicker, like trying to walk through mud. The closer I went, the thicker it felt. A foot or so away from the clock, though, was like a charged wall. I put out a finger, then pulled it back as the shock rippled through my body. A slow, careful search of the air revealed that there wasn't even a millimetre Alice hadn't covered. That countdown timer, just like the couch, was one hundred percent sealed.

Adeline tried too, but she had no more luck than I had. Just as we were ungraciously accepting defeat, I noticed it: a tabby cat, curled up on a chair close to the fireplace.

'Has he been there the whole time?'

Adeline patted the cat. 'Julian could sleep through an earthquake.'

Oh dear. Her eyes lit up when she rubbed him. She loved that lazy little guy in the same way my mother loved Mischief.

'Well, let's hope he can also sleep through being burned to death, then,' I said – perhaps not quite as sympathetically as I'd been going for. 'But let's hope even *more* that it doesn't come to that. Look, we can't get to the countdown timer. But we can't give up. Maybe you could try all of the doors and windows, Adeline. There *has* to be a weak spot somewhere. And I'll feel out the barrier around the couch.'

Adeline didn't look too confident, but she ran off to check nonetheless. I approached the couch again – well, as close as I could manage – testing the air. Just like the air around the countdown timer, there didn't seem to be so much as a millimetre of weakness.

'We've already tried, love,' said my mother. 'This spell is about as tight as they come.'

I glanced at the timer. Three minutes, five seconds to go. Well, gosh darn it anyway. *Finally* I came into my power, and now it was about to be taken away from me. In quite a painful way too, I might add.

'Tell me about the Inferno spell.'

My mother frowned. 'Really, Wanda? I think this might be one of those cases where *not* knowing is best, love.'

I grunted. 'Come *on.* Tell me. You're not seriously just going to accept this, are you? Tell me you're thinking of a plan.'

'We're trying,' said Christine. 'Really, we are. But it's like we said – Alice is a *lot* more powerful than we expected. And there are only two ways to get *that* kind of power – dark forbidden magic, or old – as in *very* old – age. I'm not sure which route Alice has gone down, but there's no way we can compete on the same level. We can't stop her Inferno spell. And the house will stay sealed until it's over. It–'

'Wait!' I interrupted. 'Stop right there. You said you can't stop it, and that it'll stay sealed till it's over. So … how long does an Inferno spell last?'

They seemed to think about it for a moment. 'About an hour, usually,' my mother replied. 'They burn incredibly hot. Water can't put them out. Nothing can. They burn till everything is destroyed, then the spell just … stops.'

'Usually,' Christine added.

'Well, let's say we give it an hour and a half, then, just to be on the safe side.' I paced the small living room, turning it all over in my mind. I could have done with another burrito, to be honest, but for the moment the cogs were turning just fine. 'So that's what we have to do, then.' I nodded to myself, realising that I was *thinking* a lot more than I was actually saying. But I understood what I meant, that was the main thing. 'Yes,' I repeated. 'That's exactly what we have to do.'

While my mother, Christine and Lassie looked on in confusion, Max jumped up, grinning at me. 'You're right, Wanda. All we have to do is make it through the Inferno!'

'Yes!' I cried, hugging him. I pulled away from him, looking at him in wonderment for a moment. Of all the people in the room who could have figured out what crazy idea I had percolating, I would *not* have bet my money on Max. 'That's exactly what I was thinking,' I said. 'Then the seal will be undone. Then we can leave.' We turned to the couch. 'Right?'

My mother and Christine exchanged somewhat dubious glances. 'Well … technically, yes,' said Christine. 'But there's just one problem. How do we survive an Inferno spell?'

I bit my lip, looking tentatively at them. Once I said this, we'd all know the truth about Wanda Wayfair. Either I was a mad genius, or I was clutching at soggy straws. I steeled myself, and spat it out. 'By making this house very, very cold.'

≈

Sometimes, things look and sound a lot easier than they are. For years I looked on enviously as my coven performed spells. It always seemed to me that they did it with the greatest of ease. Even though they swore it had taken tons of effort and study, I never quite believed them.

Well, today I finally did.

'I *can* do incredibly precise Freezing spells,' said Christine carefully. 'It's vital for me. I need to be good at it so I can preserve my visions.'

'But?'

'Why do you seem so sure that there's a but?' asked Adeline.

'Because,' I informed her, 'this is my coven. I know when there's about to be a but.'

'Well, yes, there is a bit of a but,' Christine admitted. 'Although I would have thought you'd have figured it out by now.'

'Figured it .... Oh.' I slapped a hand to my forehead, and looked at my mother, Christine and Lassie, all sitting on the couch, sealed within an incredibly powerful barrier. 'You can't do magic in there, can you?'

My mother shook her head. 'No. Or at least not in any way that'd help *you*. Christine can do a freezing spell in here all right, but it would be limited to within the barrier Alice put up around us. It would only affect me, Christine and Lassie. You know what this means, Wanda?'

I slumped back into the armchair. 'That me, Max and Adeline, are soon going to smell like barbecue, and you guys can either choose to burn along with us or to save yourselves and look on in horror while *we* burn in front of you?' Always the optimist, amn't I? 'But wait.' I sat up, looking at Adeline. 'I don't suppose you ...'

She shook her head. 'I've always been better at chronicling than actually doing. I mean, I could probably freeze something small. But a spell powerful enough to outlast an Inferno? No way.'

I slumped back again.

'That's not what I meant when I asked you if you knew what this means, Wanda,' said my mother. 'I *meant* that you'll have to do it. Christine will do her own spell for us, you'll follow her and freeze the rest of the house. I've been watching you these last few days. I think you're capable. Although–' She glanced at Adeline. '–it would be nice if the other witches in the room would at least *try* before giving up.'

Adeline's cheeks flushed. 'You're right. Of course I'll help. Christine, is there an incantation, or …?'

Christine bit her lip. 'It's a long time since I've needed one for a Freezing spell. It comes so naturally to me these days, I don't even *have* to incant. Did that sound big-headed? I didn't mean to sound big-headed.'

'Be as big-headed as you like,' my mother cut in. 'As long as you come up with the incantation that saves my daughter's life.'

Christine's teeth made a grinding noise. Not good. That was something she and Melissa did when they were incredibly nervous. 'Okay. Okay. Just give me a moment to bring it to mind.' She muttered beneath her breath, clearly trying to come up with the right words. 'Right. I've got it. But it's best that we time it so that it begins *right* before the Inferno spell. And also … your mother will be able to create a bit of inner heat so that we can survive the freeze. But I think that might be a bit too much for you to handle just yet, Wanda. So maybe you'd better go and find some warm clothes.'

I ran around the house with Adeline and Max, finding cardigans, coats and blankets. Adeline boiled the kettle and made a flask of hot chocolate, too. By the time we were back in the room, wrapped up in winter clothes, the countdown timer told us there were fifty-three seconds to go.

'Right,' said Christine. 'I *think* I've come up with an incantation to suit the situation. But I mean, we're freezing a whole house for the goddess's sake, so I hope it works. Okay.' She took a deep breath. 'Okay, repeat after me:

'Frozen things remain the same
Untouched by age, by time or flames
Frozen things stand still till thawed
By a word, or a witch, or till safeness has dawned
Frozen things withstand the fire
No matter how big, no matter how dire
In a frozen state we shall be in this house
Till the Inferno is over
Or the fire is doused.'

Nervously, Adeline and I repeated each and every one of Christine's words. As we incanted, the Inferno was already beginning. A huge ball of flame erupted from where the digital timer had been, growing outwards.

Normally, I quite like fire. There's nothing better than curling up in front of one on a winter's evening, a good book in hand, a warm drink by your side. So let's just say that this *wasn't* that sort of fire. There was nothing friendly about it – you wouldn't want to gaze into its depths and dream of things to come. Looking into *this* fire was like looking into hell.

We repeated the incantation over and over – I swear, I know those words by heart now – furiously chanting while the Inferno refused to abate.

I could feel the heat of it, stinging my skin through all of my layers of clothes. But I could feel something else, too – something coming *out* of me. From my very centre, a chill was coursing. I felt it creep out from my core, then lick along my limbs. I gasped as strands of icy filaments shot from my fingers, rushing towards the ball of flame. A look at Adeline told me that she had icy strands emitting from her fingertips, too.

Together, we sent that chill towards the flame. Soon, silvery frost was covering the flame, damping it down and dousing it before it could grow.

Max looked at me in awe. 'It's working,' he said.

I couldn't reply. I was too busy muttering the incantation, over and over through chattering teeth. But inwardly, I was just as amazed as he was. I mean, no one wants to think of themselves as a crispy corpse, do they? Now that the Freezing spell seemed to be working, I could go back to imagining myself live a long, wonderful life.

The frost crystals multiplied and multiplied, hardening quickly. Soon, every surface in the house was slick with ice, and the ground was too slippery for us to stand upon. Adeline, Max and I fell into Adeline's poor, destroyed chairs – Adeline's cat didn't so much as open an eyelid when she sat next to him – and huddled inside our coats and blankets.

My mam, Christine and Lassie didn't have the luxury of layers, so they huddled into one another, teeth chattering, while my mother stuttered out spells that would raise their body heat.

Despite the fact that the house was now, basically, a giant freezer, the Inferno spell did not let up. The flames kept erupting from the centre of the living room, over and over. We had to repeat the Freezing spell three times more. I glanced at my wristwatch every now and then, wondering how long the Inferno could possibly last. The hot chocolate was gone. My lips were blue. Max huddled closer to me, lending me some of his body heat, while Adeline grabbed onto her cat for warmth (even then, Julian stayed snoring).

One hour and eighteen minutes had passed in discomfort when Max unstuck his eyelids and nodded to where the flames had been erupting from. 'H-haven't seen any n-newcomers for a w-while,' he stammered hopefully.

'N-no. Me n-neither,' I chattered back.

Christine and my mother sat forward. My mother reached out a hand testing the air around her. 'The seal is gone!' she cried. 'The spell is over!'

I leapt towards the couch, crashing into my mother's and Christine's arms. Lassie hugged Max fiercely (I'm pretty sure I heard them woof a bit, too), and Adeline stood up and said, 'Well then … I guess it's off to the Wyrd Court.'

19.A Snitch in Time

'Um ...' Lassie twiddled her hair between her fingers. 'It's not that I don't *want* to help. I hate Alice Berry for what she's put all of us through. But you all know as well as I do ... the word of a weredog will only get us so far.'

Max growled. 'That's ridiculous, Lassie. You saw Alice enchant that human into killing Connor with the candlestick. Then Alice *threatened* you. And she admitted it to all of us, too.'

Lassie still looked unsure, and the uncomfortable truth was that I couldn't blame her. I'd only been back in the supernatural world a short time, but it was enough for me to know that things could be very, *very* unfair.

'You should go,' I said to Lassie, despite my misgivings. 'You're a witness, like Max says. And the rest of us are witnesses now, too. Alice won't get away with this. But ...' I glanced at my mother. 'Maybe while they go to the courthouse, you could take me on a little detour first?'

≈

The Wyrd Court was closed to travelling, meaning that you couldn't simply click your fingers and wind up inside. It seemed like a sensible enough measure, but for our purposes just then, it was an extremely inconvenient one.

Our detour had already taken far longer than I'd hoped. By the time my mother clicked her fingers and landed us on the steps of the Wyrd Court, the trial was already in progress. My powers of observation, and the sign on the closed door that said *Trial in Progress* was what clued me in to the fact. The crowd outside the court was enormous. Wyrd News's Sandra was there, looking even skinnier and more big-haired than she did on TV.

'It's unusual for a trial to take place so soon after the plea hearing,' she said to the camera. 'But in the case of Mildred Valentine, I doubt the Wyrd Court could afford to wait. Not even Wyrd News Nightly has been granted access to this trial, but we've heard word that things are really hotting up inside, with the arrival of a surprise witness …'

We pushed past the crowd and banged on the door. A moment later, a tall, broad Peacemaker glared through. 'Oh yay, it's more Wayfairs,' he said. Somewhere beneath his helmet, I think he wrinkled his nose. 'Just what this trial needs.'

My mother squared up to him. 'I'll have none of your nonsense, young man. Stand aside.'

'Can't. No one else is allowed in. Trial's in progress.' He took a look at her brooch – a new addition. Wisely, he said nothing.

My mother narrowed her eyes and placed her hands on her hips. Good Gretel, no one in their right mind would refuse her when she looked like that. 'I can't really blame you. It's not your fault that Peacemakers aren't required to study Magical Law. But *had* you gained a degree, then you would know that it is against the law for the Wyrd Court to refuse entry to a Wayfair. At *any* time. So move aside.'

The burly guard opened the door, and we pushed past him. 'Is that true?' I whispered.

My mother shrugged. 'It is for now. But I have a feeling they'll be changing that particular law after today.'

The building was huge, with signs for countless government offices leading off the main hall. Luckily, my mother knew where the courtroom was, and we dashed along as fast as our legs could carry us.

Although we burst through the doors as loudly and dramatically as we could manage, not a single head turned in our direction.

'So much for making an entrance,' said my mother.

The courtroom wasn't nearly as thronged as the street outside, but it was far, far louder. And poor Lassie seemed to be taking the brunt of the anger. People were on their feet, shouting out obscenities at her. A box of dog biscuits flew through the air, whacking her square on the forehead.

'Come *on*!' I cried. 'Where did they even get them? Lassie's a surprise witness. How could they possibly have known that she was going to be here?'

My mother sighed. 'They didn't need to know. Materialization spell. I ought to materialize a boil the size of the moon on whoever threw them at the poor girl.' As her eyes scanned the crowd I had no doubt that, if she found the culprit, she would be as good as her word.

I took in the scene. There was an auburn-haired judge seated behind a long, polished bench. She wore full robes in a nice shade of purple, and her ceremonial witch hat sat askew on her head as she furiously pounded her gavel. 'I will have *quiet* while the witness gives her evidence. Any more antics, and I'll throw you all out. I'm looking at *you,* lawyers.'

She glared down at the benches below her. A lawyer who I sensed was a witch sat back in her seat, pocketing a rubber ball she had been about to throw. Her fellow lawyers pocketed various chew toys, balls and – I narrowed my eyes – yet another box of dog biscuits.

'*They're* the lawyers for the prosecution,' said my mother, pointing her finger at the one with the dog biscuits. 'Each and every one of them is employed by the Wyrd Court. It's their job to prove Mildred guilty.' As her finger stayed pointing, the dog-biscuit thrower suddenly developed a very large, red lump on the tip of his nose.

I scanned the courtroom for faces I knew. Adeline, Christine and Max were sitting just behind the second table of lawyers – the vampires, judging by their pallor and dramatic make-up (yes, vampires *do* like dark red lipstick and black eyeliner – some things are clichés because they're true). Mildred's husband Basil was sitting next to the vampire lawyers. He wore a slightly different pair of sunglasses, but other than that he looked very much the same as he had when his tongue was down Alice Berry's throat – in other words, he still made my skin crawl.

On the other side of the court, I saw Will Berry sitting next to his aunt and a row of people I guessed were other Berrys. Alice was wringing her fingers, glaring at Lassie, Adeline, Christine and Max.

Mildred Valentine was seated close to the front of the court, for all to see. Her chair was raised up a little, and there was a strange haze surrounding her.

'It's called a Vampire-Proof … thingy. Extra barriers are needed with vampires,' my mother whispered as we found some empty seats close to the front. 'This way, she won't be able to vaporize or turn into a bat.'

I nodded absentmindedly, keeping my eye on my mother's brooch. 'It's all right,' I whispered. 'Not long now.'

The brooch emitted a sound that was just a *little* on the huffy side.

'I have a feeling he's losing his patience,' I said. 'Should we let him out now?'

'Maybe,' my mother replied. 'Oh, wait. Things are calming down. That lawyer is saying something.'

The judge's gavel pounding had relaxed. She fixed one of the lawyers with a wary glare and said, 'Go on with what you were saying, Mr Rundt. Oh, and just in case you forget again – you are *not* a performer. This is a courtroom, not the stage. So just do your job and stick to the facts.'

Mr Rundt gave the judge an obsequious smile and turned to the jury. Just like the lawyers for the prosecution, each and every member of the jury was a witch. Given that the defendant was a vampire, it hardly seemed like the fairest of set-ups.

'A few minutes ago,' Mr Rundt began. 'We thought this trial over and done with. We have a defendant with motive, opportunity and – let's not forget – a whole lot of evidence to mark her as the murderer. Why *wouldn't* we think it was all wrapped up? I don't know about you guys, but I was getting ready to go home to my bed and my cocoa – or maybe my brandy, eh?' He winked and the jurors laughed. 'But then a *Wayfair* arrived. And with her, she brought this weredog.' He turned from the jury and sneered at Lassie. 'Now, I'm not seated where you are. I can't make up your minds for you. But let's consider this. At the very last moment, a weredog appears from *nowhere* and tells us that not only is Mildred Valentine *not* guilty, but that the beloved and respected Alice Berry *is.* I mean … seriously?'

The jury laughed.

Lassie let out a low growl. 'I *didn't* say that Alice alone was responsible. I told you her boyfriend – Mildred's husband – was behind it too. And I also told you that Alice Berry admitted it all to me *and* three Wayfairs *and* a chronicler and my cousin Max this afternoon. Just what is it that you're having trouble believing?'

The lawyer raised a brow at the jury. 'Weredogs, am I right?'

The jury laughed. The judge pounded her gavel once more. 'What did I say about performing, Mr Rundt? This is a serious proceeding,' she said. 'I will *not* have you making little jokes to woo the jury.' She cleared her throat. 'However, despite the annoying way he went about it, Mr Rundt did make some valid points. In the case against Mildred Valentine, we have evidence. Real evidence. But in the case for her defence, we have only the word of a weredog.'

'And a chronicler and a Wayfair and another weredog!' Christine shouted out.

More uproar ensued. This was getting ridiculous. No, this had gone past ridiculous and was heading into an altogether different realm. *This* was the world I'd finally been allowed to enter? It didn't seem quite so shiny and wonderful anymore. I stood up, pulled the brooch from my mother's bodice, and approached the judge.

'Actually!' I shouted. 'I have another witness right here!'

Finally, the courtroom grew quiet as, in my hands, the brooch began to grow. Within seconds, Mike the accountant was standing on the floor beside me, a ream of paper and a box of videotapes in his hands.

'And who are you?' asked Judge Redvein.

'Mike Griffin,' he said quietly. 'Formerly the accountant to the Berry Coven. I'm the one Alice made plant Mildred Valentine's fingerprints all over Berrys' Bottlers. *And* she made me plant the Berry Good Go Juice recipe in Mildred's house. And I also have all of the missing security footage from each and every attack, *plus* the footage from Berrys' Bottlers which will prove there never was a break-in, plus …'

As Mike listed the evidence he'd brought with him, Alice Berry stood up. 'You dirty little snitch,' she screamed. 'I should have killed you too.' She rounded on me, pointing a finger. I ducked as a bolt of red-hot lightning came my way. Luckily, it only singed my hair. The judge's bench took the brunt.

The judge's voice sounded again, but this time it positively boomed. I guess there was some magic involved, but either way, *no* one could have failed to hear her as she called out, 'Peacemakers! Arrest Alice Berry this instant. Alice Berry, you are charged with the murders of Eoin Reynolds, Connor Cramer and Maureen O'Mara, as well as seventeen other attacks. You are *also* charged with the attempted murder of three Wayfairs, two weredogs and a chronicler.'

As I watched a group of incredibly large Peacemakers surge towards the Berrys, I couldn't help but notice that Will was looking right at me. I'd like to say his eyes were filled with love and admiration, but I'd be lying through my teeth. In truth, the look that Will was shooting my way was impossible to fathom.

I turned to the judge. 'I think you've forgotten someone.'

She stared blankly back.

'Basil Valentine? He and Alice were in on it together. He turned himself into a big slimy pile of vapoury stuff and whispered the trigger words in quite a few of the attacks. I'm *pretty* sure Lassie told you all this in the witness stand.'

Lassie nodded. 'I did. No one listened.'

The judge reddened, pounded her gavel and her voice became surround-sound once more. 'Also, arrest Basil Valentine!'

The Peacemakers broke into two groups, one dragging Alice kicking and screaming through a door at the back of the courtroom, the other heading for Basil Valentine. Unfortunately, he hadn't been surrounded with a magical Vampire-Proof thingy like his wife had. Before the Peacemakers could reach him, he turned into a swirl of vapour. If I squinted, I could *just* about see him. The Peacemakers tried desperately to grasp onto him, but he slipped through every time. A few of them rose into the air, using flying-potions and brooms, chasing him down.

I wasn't feeling at *all* smug when I spied the look of embarrassment on Judge Redvein's face as Peacemaker after Peacemaker failed to catch Basil. I'm sure my mother was feeling equally un-smug when she approached the bench, leaned closer to the judge and said, 'Y'know, I might just know a Wayfair who'd be able to catch him. Pity we can't get warrants to arrest vampires, isn't it?'

Judge Redvein scowled. 'Fine,' she said through gritted teeth. 'You have the warrant.'

'Christine!' my mother called across the courtroom. 'We have the warrant to arrest Basil! Time for you to do your stuff.'

With a slightly crazed grin on her face, Christine stood up, focused on Basil's vapour (why does that sound far ickier than it is?) and began to mumble.

20.Goodbye Old Familiar

I left the courtroom before the others, stopping briefly to thank Mike for all he'd done. He hadn't exactly been pleased to see me when I turned up on his doorstep with my mother in tow. But after I told him about Alice's attempt to murder Lassie, he knew he could well be next. If Alice was getting rid of anyone who knew what she'd done, then Mike would be *very* high on that list.

We had hoped that Mike wouldn't have to testify. In an ideal world, the jury would have taken Lassie at her word, and Mike could have kept himself off the Berrys' radar. But the world of the supernatural was as far from ideal as the human world. Even when my mother and I asked Mike to come 'just in case' we both knew he would certainly be needed. So she had done what she refused to do to her familiar – she had charmed him into a brooch.

My mother worked even more magic before we ever took Mike to the Wyrd Court. Protection spells had been set around his house, and Mike and his family should be safe from any retribution the Berrys' might think of enacting. We promised him that the Wayfairs would always keep an eye on him, just in case.

After my brief goodbye to Mike, my mother told the others that we'd join them back at the coven's house soon. First, I needed her to take me back to my own place.

≈

I took her hand and held on tight while she clicked her fingers. When we arrived back in my bedroom, I thought we were too late.

I rushed towards the chair next to my bed. 'No, Dudley!' I cried, snuggling into his tiny, stinking body. 'I wanted to say goodbye.'

He opened an eye, making both my mother and me scream out loud.

'Good Gretel!' cried my mother. 'We thought you were …'

He fluffed his little cotton ball pillow and sat up. 'Not quite,' he said, his voice weak. 'But it won't be long. I can feel it happening. And seeing as I'm dying, I guess that means that you finally caught Maureen's murderer?'

I nodded. 'Alice has been arrested. Basil almost got away, but Christine froze him just in time. It's all over, Dudley.'

He closed his eyes, let out a little sigh, and said, 'Thank you both. Maureen was right about you, Wanda. You're the real–' He paused on a stuttering breath. 'The real … deal.'

With those words, he stopped moving.

'Are you messing with us, Dudley?' I asked shakily. 'Are you going to open your eyes again and make us jump out of our skins?'

He still didn't move. My mother gently touched his tiny body. 'There's no heartbeat, Wanda,' she told me. 'Nothing at all. I think he's really dead.'

With a shaky hand, I stroked his body. She was right. There was no sign of life. 'Dudley's not dead,' I told her. 'He's just gone to join his witch.' And while I said it, for some stupid reason, I was wiping away tears.

≈

I hadn't been to Riddler's Cove since the Winter Solstice before last – or was it the one before that? Either way, it was time to stop avoiding the place where I was born. Even I knew that it was customary to bury a familiar next to their witch, and I was *not* going to let Dudley down.

'I'll take you there,' said my mother. 'I know the graveyard in Riddler's Cove all too well.'

I looked down at Dudley's little body. 'I'd like you to go with me, but I think … I think it's time I finally learned to travel myself. I'm going to try clicking my fingers. I think it's what Dudley – and Maureen O'Mara – would want.'

My mother smiled. 'I think you're right. But you've not learned how to travel to particular coordinates yet. Do you remember the graveyard well enough to bring the image to mind?'

'No.' It shamed me to admit it, but I visited my father's grave as little as possible. I hadn't been there for years and, when I *did* go, I just felt like I was talking to an empty casket. Probably because I *was* talking to an empty casket; his body had never been found. 'But there's somewhere I remember *really* well. The field behind our house? Can we both go there and walk the rest of the way to the graveyard.'

Her eyes grew a little misty. I knew her memories of that field were just as fond as mine. That was where my father used to test-fly his brooms. Sometimes we'd spread out a picnic blanket and sit there, watching him as he soared into the sky.

She nodded. 'I think it's the perfect destination for your first attempt. You go first, and I'll follow behind.'

I picked Dudley up, placing him gently in the crook of my arm. With the image of that beautiful field in my mind, I clicked my finger.

≈

The sun was setting over Riddler's Cove when I arrived. The field was full of early-ripened barley, shining golden in the sunset. Being there after all these years brought a strange, constricted feeling to my chest. I missed my father more than I cared to admit.

Luckily, my mother arrived straight after me, saving me from my tears. 'You did it,' she told me, her face shining with pride. 'Today, on your twenty-first birthday of all times, you've performed an incredibly complicated freezing spell, put two murderers in prison, and travelled all by yourself for the very first time. Not bad for a witch who thought she'd never get her power.'

I shrugged. 'I could give you some humble brag or other in response, but let's just bury Dudley and get back for the party.'

She wrapped her arm around me, and we made our way through Riddler's Cove. The stores I remembered were all shut for the evening. I looked longingly into the window of Caulfield's Cakes. Now that I could travel at the click of a finger, I'd be eating a *lot* more unhealthily.

The tavern, a place called *Three Witches Brew* was the only business still open at that hour. There were a few witches seated outside, enjoying an evening drink.

When I was a child, *Three Witches Brew* had been the only tavern in town. If that was still the case, then it meant it was where Will had bought that broom. I was just about to tell my mother about the broom when she said, 'Here we are. Just on the hill.'

She opened a rickety wooden gate and entered the Witches' Graveyard. The hill was low and wide. From the side we approached, we had a view of the whole town. It was larger than I remembered. I could see the huge mansions on the east side, juxtaposed by our own old house, closer to the hill. I'd never thought much about it when I was a kid, but looking at Wayfarers' Rest now, I realised just how much magic was holding my childhood home together. Like Crooked College, the upper floors were *far* too wide to be supported by the floors below. And yet there it stood, immovable and – in its own way – the most perfect house in the world.

We found Maureen's grave on the west side of the hill. A hawthorn tree shaded her from the sun, and there was a stunning view of the sea, sparkling in the last of the evening's light. There was a tiny grave right next to hers, already dug.

'He'll be happy here,' I said, taking in a deep breath of salty air.

'Yes,' my mother agreed. 'They both will.'

I might have cried just a little bit at that. My mother even shed a tear or two herself. It's funny how a stinking, toothless rat can have that effect on you.

≈

The rest of the night was one big, exhausting blur. When we returned to Westerly Crescent, my party was already in full swing. I mean, who says the guest of honour even has to *be* there?

'Your empowerment ceremony will have to wait for a few days,' my mother told me as we walked in together. 'It has to be a private ceremony. Just the coven. It's better with a full moon, too. And I don't know about you, but I don't fancy my chances at sending any of *this* lot back to their own homes just yet.'

She was right. The party guests were merry, to say the least. And seeing as the table was laden with drinks, cakes and snacks it'd probably be quite some time before they were ready to call it a night.

So I did the only thing I could. I let the guests cry out, 'Happy birthday, Wanda!' And then I tucked into cake, drank fizzy wine and orange juice, and thanked the stars that it was all over.

Max and Lassie were there, as well as Rover and a few other weredogs. Melissa brought some friends from Crooked College, and my mother and Christine had filled the house with family friends. Adeline couldn't make the party, unfortunately. She had told Christine that she had to go home and feed her cat. I almost wished I could be there to watch. *Could* a cat eat and sleep at the same time? If there was a way, no doubt Julian would find it.

I might have glanced at my phone once or twice (or a hundred times) during the party. But there was no message from Will. Had I really expected there to be? More to the point, had I really *wanted* there to be?

21.Dizzy

The next morning I woke to find Lassie's door open, and her room cleared out. I made my way downstairs and found Max sitting dejectedly on the bottom step.

'You okay?' I nudged him gently.

'Will be,' he croaked. 'She got a lift to Riddler's Cove on the back of some witch's broom last night. Told me she needed a break from Dublin. Too many memories of Connor.'

'I can understand that.' I really could. After my visit to the graveyard at Riddler's Cove the night before, I had come to realise that my long absence from my coven's life had just as much to do with grief over my father as it had to do with sour grapes.

He stood up, reaching out a hand to help me up. 'Anyway, I'll stop being depressed now. We have to go and do our maintenance minutes.' He hesitated. 'Although … you don't *really* look like you're up to it. Do you wanna go back to bed?'

'Good Gretel, yes,' I admitted. 'But I'm not going to.'

'Too much to drink?'

I shook my head. 'Too much to study. '

After the party was over, and Max, Lassie and I stumbled back to our own house, I'd felt far too wired for sleep. At four in the morning, I'd clicked my fingers into Melissa's room, nabbed one of her Magical Law textbooks, and travelled back to my own room again to read it. I'd scoured through the chapters, learning everything I could about Wayfairs, Peacemakers and the Wyrd Court. When my alarm clock went off at seven, I hadn't even been to bed.

'Come on,' I said. 'Let's get this over with – and then I'll take you to the Water Bowl for a breakfast burrito.'

'With extra tofu scramble?' His mouth watered.

I withheld my laughter. 'Extra anything you like, you wonderful vegan weredog.'

≈

Max took the clippers from my hands. 'I'll finish off this hedge,' he said. 'You look like you need a break.'

I sat back on the grass for a moment, watching him cut into the hedge. I'd made a bit of a mess of it, to be honest. It was almost bald in more than one spot. We'd been at our maintenance minutes for – I glanced at my watch – fifty-three minutes now. Already I was tiring. The wizards who normally let Max borrow their gadgets were all working that morning, so we'd had to wrench open the door of the garden shed, and pull out Max's rusty lawnmower and clippers.

Still, I thought, now that Max was evening out the hedge for me, my morning's work didn't look *too* bad. And Luna Park was lovely at this hour. Green and gorgeous and quiet. There were only a few people out – some witches doing a yoga class on the east side, and some dayturners sitting on a bench closer to us, sharing a bottle of something that looked a little too viscous to be red wine. I wasn't sure which should disturb me more – drinking alcohol this early in the morning, or drinking … something else.

'So when do you think you'll move on?' Max's voice startled me out of my reverie.

'Move on? Who says I'm moving?' I pointed to a cloud that was hovering above. 'Doesn't that one look a bit like Rover?'

Max laid the clippers aside and sat down next to me, peering up at the sky. 'Oh yeah,' he agreed. 'It's got his ears. But seriously, when are you leaving?'

I turned over to look at him. 'You trying to get rid of me so soon? You know, you could give a girl a complex.'

'Give over,' he grunted. 'I just thought … isn't that what Wayfairs do? Wander around, fighting wayward witches and supernaturals and putting the world to rights.'

'Oh.' I plucked a daisy from the grass. 'I guess. Except it's only witches these days, thanks to the Minister for Magical Law. Seriously, though – do you want me to move?'

'No!' He said it a little more vehemently than he intended, I imagine, because his face grew pink and he suddenly became interested in a nearby elder tree. 'I mean

… I'm getting used to you. And Lassie won't be back for a while. So … the house'll be kind of big and lonely.'

I felt sad for him. In the short time I'd seen him interact with his cousin, it had been obvious that they were close. I was sure that, once she'd grieved for Connor, she'd come back to Westerly Crescent again. But as for me …?

'Well …' I began cautiously. How could I tell Max I loved living with him without inflating his ego too much? 'Westerly Crescent's not *so* bad, I suppose. I have kind of grown fond of plant milk. So there's that.'

He shot me a tentative grin. 'And there's the pens, too. Don't forget about the pens. You'll never run out of pens as long as you live with me.'

I was just about to quip back, when I noticed Max's grin had faded. He'd shifted himself from his comfortable cloud-gazing position, and was sitting up, shielding his eyes and looking at the east side of the park.

I sat up, too. When I saw what he was looking at, my throat went dry and my hands grew clammy. Good Gretel, why couldn't bodily fluids just make a decision and stick to it?

'Here comes Will,' Max said tonelessly. 'Yay. Do you want me to stay?'

My mind struggled to reach so much as a gentle walk. I told you, without food my thought process is next to useless. I glanced from Will to Max, shrugging. 'Do what you like. I doubt it's going to be a romantic conversation.'

Max sighed, stood up and said, 'I'll be a few feet away. I think I missed a bit of grass when I cut it earlier.'

I resisted the urge to grab onto him for dear life, and let him go. He left the clippers next to me, and pushed the lawnmower a few feet away. I stood up, brushing grass off my jeans, watching Will's progress. Maybe he wasn't even coming to see me. Maybe he was just out for a nice Saturday morning stroll.

'Hi!' shouted Will. Shouting was necessary, because Max had just started the engine on the mower. Good goddess, that thing was in need of a tune up. Next time I saw the wizards, I'd ask them to give it a check. Actually, next time I saw the wizards I'd ask them where I could buy some of their gadgets.

'Hi!' I shouted back, wishing I didn't feel so sick. The three slices of birthday cake I'd eaten last night suddenly seemed like overindulgence. I wasn't so sure I could handle a breakfast burrito anymore.

'Do you want to go somewhere quieter?' shouted Will.

'Sure!' I shouted back.

We looked around. The dayturners had finished their bottle of red fluid and were sauntering out of the park. We took a seat on the bench they had vacated.

And then we sat there … and sat there … and sat there …

Finally, Will broke the silence. 'Is it true then? What Auntie Alice said? Were you just using me? Spying on me?'

'Oh.' I stared down at my hands. I was still clutching the daisy I'd picked earlier, and by now I'd squashed the poor thing. 'So we're just going to get straight to the point. Well, no. And yes.'

He clenched his jaw. 'Which is it, Wanda?'

'Both. Look, Will … I *was* investigating the murders. And I did want to find out what the Berry Good Go Juice had to do with it all. Turns out, a lot. But I wasn't investigating the whole time. When I got the job, I had no idea about the murders, or even that you and Alice were witches. I swear.'

He narrowed his eyes. 'And when *did* you know, exactly? When did you start investigating me, Wanda? Was it before we had dinner together, or after?'

'Before,' I admitted. 'But Will, that doesn't mean–' I stopped midsentence, with no idea how to finish.

'Oh.' He blinked. 'So … when I gave you that broom, and told you my deepest, darkest secret, you were already investigating my coven?'

I looked away from him. I had to. His gorgeous sea-green eyes were shining. He looked beyond upset with me. 'I can give you back the broom if you want.'

'Keep it,' he said. 'When I said I wanted you to have it, I meant it. I'm not a two-faced Wayfair like you.'

'Will.' I tried to reach out a hand, but he shifted along the bench. 'Will, please. I know what I did was hurtful, but you *must* be able to see that I had my reasons. Your aunt *was* a murderer. She hypno-potioned those poor humans into murdering innocent witches. Oh, yeah – and she tried to murder me and some of my family and friends, too.'

He met my eyes. 'I know, and I'm sorry. I told her that was wrong. No matter what was at stake she should never have hurt you. And I do want you to know something.' He kept his gaze steady on mine. There they were – those darned fluttery feelings, all over again. 'I had no part in it. In any of it. I had *no* idea. Do you believe me?'

'I'm pretty sure your aunt would have taken great delight in telling me if you were,' I said. 'Y'know, when she was getting ready to murder me.'

'Yeah, she probably would have.' He sighed. 'But Wanda, this isn't about my aunt. This is about you and me. I liked you. I mean … proper liked you. Big deal liked you. It hit me like a brick, the second I met you at that job interview. And I thought you liked me back. I thought you were the most honest girl I'd ever met. But now … I don't think I'll ever be able to believe a word you say, ever again.'

For a brief moment I considered doing *exactly* what my feelings wanted me to do – I wanted to grab him and kiss him. Kiss him until he kissed me back. Kiss him until he knew that, no matter what might have happened in the past few days, the way I felt about him had been real.

And it had. It had been big, and bright, and almost impossible to resist. But only *almost.* Because no matter how gorgeous he was, no matter how he made my skin tingle and my heart flutter … he was a Berry, and I was a Wayfair. He didn't see the world in the same way I did, and I wasn't sure if he ever would.

So when he stood up from the bench and began to walk away … I just let him.

'Oh, and also,' he called back over his shoulder as he stalked towards the east side of the park, 'you probably don't need me to tell you this, but you're fired.'

'Well,' I muttered to myself. 'That went well.'

I didn't watch Will's form disappear. Because let's face it, a girl can only have so much self-restraint, and the back of Will was at *least* as gorgeous as the front.

So after a couple of minutes of gazing at the ground, I left the bench and walked towards Max. Sure, going home and licking my wounds would have been preferable, but Max had already done more than enough by himself.

'You have a rest,' I told him as I approached. 'I'll finish off here and then we'll go to the Water Bowl.'

'You sure? Because if you'd rather just be by yourself …' He was looking *way* too closely at me.

'I'm sure,' I said, prising the lawnmower from his grip.

He let go of the handle, and the motor cut out. Just as I was about to start the motor up again, something hit me square on the head.

I looked up, rubbing my head. Then I looked down.

'It's a bat,' said Max, pointing at the small brownish-black creature on the ground. 'Wow, it's a good thing the motor wasn't running. This little guy could have been a gonner.'

I shuddered at the thought.

'Bit early in the day for a bat to be out,' Max went on. His eyes suddenly filled with panic. 'What if it's a vampire, Wanda? What if it's Basil or some crony of his, come for revenge?'

I bent down to the bat, reaching out. It was warm, but it wasn't moving. 'Well if it is, he's not doing a very good job of it, is he? Maybe we should take it to a vet.'

'No thanks,' said a faint, squeaky voice. 'I'll be okay in a minute.'

Max and I gaped as one at the bat. By now, we shouldn't have been surprised when an animal decided to speak, but apparently we were a little slow on the uptake today.

The bat sat up. 'I'm Dizzy.'

'Of course you are, you poor thing,' I said soothingly. 'Can we get you anything? A drink? Something to eat?'

'No.' The bat shook its head. 'I mean, my name is Dizzy. And I'm really not up to flying anymore, so *please* tell me I've found you. Please tell me you're Wanda Wayfair?'

I groaned. 'I am. Why?'

Dizzy extended a … a something. 'Oh, thank the blessed Lord of mangoes. You're the one. The Wayfarer. You're going to help me solve my witch's murder. But first … I think I need to go and have a lie upside down.'

≈

You've reached the end of *Bottling It.* I hope you enjoyed this read. If so, join my mailing list to keep up with the very latest releases: http://www.subscribepage.com/z4n0f4

Or visit: https://aaalbright.com and sign up there.

Bricking It, the second Wayfair Witches' Mystery is available to download or buy now. And if you'd like to find out a little more about the inhabitants of Wanda's world, turn the page to find *An Extract From the Compendium of Supernatural Beings.*

Extract from the Compendium of Supernatural Beings

Edition 5001.
Year of Publication: the Year of the Lotus (otherwise known as 2017 AD).
Chronicler: Adeline A. Albright (Senior Chronicler and Librarian, Crooked College, Warren Lane, Dublin 2)

Major Supernatural Beings

Witches:

Witches, both male and female, are considered the most magical of supernatural beings. Their power is innate and (almost always) inherited. It would not be possible to list all witch abilities in this compendium, however many witches choose to specialize in one particular area. In the Year of the Lizard (2016 AD), the most popular subject at Crooked College was Materialization. The Society for Senior Witches stated that this was 'indicative of an unfortunate downward decline in morality.'

Most witches belong to covens. Whilst each family may legally form a coven of its own, it is more usual for the smaller, newer witch families to join the covens of the larger, more established families.

There has been criticism from other supernatural factions in recent years, driven by what many refer to as the 'elitist attitude of witches'. Whilst all supernatural enclaves (sub-dimensional regions) are accessible by witches, the witches keep their own enclaves strictly private. Mildred Valentine, currently running for the presidency of the Irish vampire enclaves, has stated that, if she gets into power, she will do her 'utmost to uncover the secrecy surrounding witch enclaves, and ensure that all enclaves are accessible to all supernatural communities.'

Warlocks:

The warlock movement has been around for centuries. It began in the Year of the Snout (2001 B.C), when a small group of male witches formed the Warlock Society. Their original manifesto has been lost to the ages, but it is widely accepted that their modern manifesto is representative of the society's early beliefs: that men are unfairly represented within the matriarchal structure of witch society, and recognition of their unique male capabilities is important to society as a whole.

Because warlocks are, genetically speaking, witches, they are free to access all witch enclaves.

Wizards:

(Note: This edition of the Compendium is the first to include wizards in the Major Supernatural Beings section. To find references to wizards in previous compendia, the chronicler suggests you begin looking under the section labelled: Others)

Wizards can be male, female, or anything else they like. They are also known as mages, shamans and wiccans, and are often overlooked. This is due to the fact that wizards are almost always of human origin. Their power is neither innate, nor inherited. A wizard's power is hard won and, because of that, this chronicler feels they should be treated with respect instead of derision.

With no access to any of the major magical enclaves, tomes or educational facilities, wizards have nevertheless managed to study and (in many cases) perfect the art of magic. They have become expert at harnessing and directing the elements, and utilising OUPs (objects of unusual power), OAPs (objects of awesome power), AUPs (areas of unusual power) and AAPs (areas of awesome power).

Wizards traditionally reside in the human enclaves, most often working in science and technology – though a small few run candle stores, yoga studios, holistic centres and the like. In recent years, witches have – somewhat – relaxed their attitude to wizards. Wizards are now free to work in witch enclaves (wearing a Pendant of Privilege), but they may not reside there (although they are entitled to reside in the enclaves specifically open to *others*).

These days, many wizards can be found working in the magical devices sector. A growing number of witches are choosing wizard-made brooms.

Mages: See entry for Wizards

Shamans: See entry for Wizards

Wiccans: See entry for Wizards

Werewolves:

Werewolves are an example to us all that, with the right attitude, you can make a curse work *for* you. There are many conflicting chronicles of how, when and why these beings were hexed. Werewolves themselves have a long-standing policy of neither confirming nor denying any single chronicle.

What we do know is this: during the full moon (and including the day preceding and the day following said moon) all werewolves transform from their humanoid body, becoming wolves for three consecutive nights. But though the change lasts for three nights, *during* these nights it begins at sunset and ends at sundown. Because of this, the transformation tends not to affect werewolves in their daily lives.

The werewolf curse can be passed on via a simple bite or scratch to any part of the body. The curse has many upsides: unusual strength, longevity (some werewolves have been known to live as long as vampires) and good looks. Rigorous testing has proved that even the ugliest human or witch, when transformed into a werewolf, instantly becomes more attractive.

The lure of werewolf-hood is irresistible to many witches. The well-known actress Veronica Berry has recently chosen to be turned by her werewolf lover, lead guitarist with the Call of the Wild. In a statement to *Young Witch Weekly,* Veronica said, 'I've been told ad-nauseam that there's a danger of losing quite a large chunk of my power. Do I care? No. Not when there's so much sexiness to gain.'

Fans have been speculating that Veronica – already considered an incredibly beautiful witch – will become the best-looking witch in history after the turn.

Veronica is not alone in her feelings about werewolves. In the last year alone, a thousand Pendants of Privilege have been issued to werewolves, allowing them to enter the witch enclaves. The Call of the Wild, and a number of other werewolf rock bands, regularly perform concerts there.

Vampires:

Like the werewolf curse, there are many conflicting chronicles of the origins of vampirism. Many vampires have submitted themselves for testing, and recent findings confirm that vampirism is, indeed, a blood-borne virus – albeit a virus with extremely unusual behaviour. The blood of a vampire is both a poison and an antidote.

Often a human will resist a vampire bite. This is, frankly, the most foolish thing they could do. A willing *bitee* (as the vampires refer to them) will be drained by only a minor amount. Full penetration of the vein will do no damage whatsoever, and may even give the *bitee* a burst of energy equal to a strong cup of coffee or a shot of ginseng. After the bite, the vampire will perform a simple act of hypnotism, thus striking the event from the *bitees* memory and leaving them with nothing but a spring in their step.

If the human resists and manages to escape before full penetration, a vampire bite can leave the victim feeling weak for days. Often humans will complain of flu-like symptoms.

The process of becoming a vampire is a little more complicated than becoming a werewolf: in order to turn, you must drink a vampire's blood before sunset on the day following the original bite. It is always preferable to drink from the vampire who administered the bite. Drinking from a different vampire can result in many complications (further details of which can be found in the Compendium of Supernatural Ailments). In recent years, the most common complication arising from such turnings has been the virus known as *Dayturning* (see Dayturner entry below).

Benefits of the vampire virus include: increased strength; near-perfect health (a small number of humans and witches with terminal illnesses resort to vampirism in order to cure their illness. In the majority of cases, the vampire virus does, indeed, provide a cure); ability to transform into a bat; ability to transform into a nearly-invisible vapour; ability to hypnotise; telepathy (the telepathic link can generally be established from vampire to vampire only, however there have been cases of vampires who can read the minds of all creatures); long lifespan.

Problems associated with the vampire virus include: blood-drinking as the main source of nutrition (a small subset of vampires who were vegetarian in their previous life have set up the No Food with a Face Foundation. They are currently researching many alternatives to blood. Promising results have been seen with a vitamin popular in the human world, known as B12); sensitivity to daylight (although the hat and sunglasses sector is quite happy about this); long lifespan.

Dayturners:

(Note: in previous compendia, dayturners were listed in the *Others* section)

A hitherto rare being, dayturners are becoming more and more common, with fifty new dayturners registered in the Year of the Lizard (2016 AD). Dayturners are vampires who feel the need to feed by daylight, and are incredibly sensitive to the dark. Feeding at night leaves them with serious indigestion (often resulting in hospitalisation). Additionally, venturing outside after sunset results in a rapidly spread rash, for which there is no known cure. Recent findings revealed that the dayturner virus is activated primarily by careless turning practices (drinking from a vampire other than the one who administered the bite). Research into a cure has been suspended due to lack of funding.

Weredogs:

(Note: in previous compendia, weredogs were listed in the *Others* section)

Like werewolves, the shifting of a human into a dog is controlled by the full moon, but instead of transforming into a supernatural variation of *Canis Lupus Lupus,* they transform into any of the many breeds of *Canis Lupus Familiaris*. There is little known about the origin of the species. In the Year of the Cat (2010 AD), outspoken vampire politician Mildred Valentine claimed to have been sent evidence that the weredogs are descendants of werewolves, having come about as the result of long-ago trysts between werewolves and *Canis Lupus Familiaris*. Both werewolves and weredogs hotly deny this. However, neither side will agree to DNA testing. As for the evidence Mildred Valentine allegedly received? She has refused to produce it, stating that doing so would endanger her source.

Familiars:

Familiars are animals with limited magical capabilities. They usually reside with witches. A witch does not choose her familiar. The familiar chooses the witch. The most common familiar animals are cats, though other animals have been known. The most notable magical ability of a familiar is the ability to communicate in any language it chooses – thus, familiars may communicate freely with their witches. They *have* been known to converse with other supernatural beings, but only when they want to. Speaking with humans is rarer still for familiars, but not unheard of.

The Unempowered:

Not to be confused with the disempowered, the unempowered witch is, like the wizards, far too often overlooked. In fact, unempowered is a modern term, and will not be found in compendia earlier than the Year of the Cat (2010 AD). Before then, there was no word for these witches. Officially, they did not exist. In the compendia dating from the Year of the Cat to the Year of the Lizard (2010-2016 AD) you will find the unempowered under the listing: Others.

In rare cases, a witch is empowered from the moment of conception, but most do not display any signs of power until a little later (five or six is the norm). The very latest that any witch has been known to come into their power is twenty-one. If they have not been empowered by then, they never will.

Unempowered witches can live in the witch enclaves if they so wish, but only with the use of a Pendant of Privilege. Even then, their access is restricted – not by other witches, but by the simple fact that they do not have the capability.

Most unempowered feel (understandably) excluded, and turn away from supernatural life, choosing to live in human enclaves instead. It is becoming more popular for unempowered witches to study wizardry.

The Disempowered:

A disempowered witch is a witch who has been stripped of all power, as a result of crimes committed. This can only occur by decree of the Wyrd Court. The length of disempowerment depends on the crime in question. In serious cases, a witch may be disempowered for life.

Books by A.A. Albright

All of my books are set in the same magical world, with the same magical rules and supernaturals occurring throughout. Each series itself is self-contained, and you don't need to read any one series to understand another. But my characters do reserve the right to pop in on one another from time to time to make a little cameo or two.

Books in the Wayfair Witches Series:

Book One: Bottling It
Book Two: Bricking It
Book Three: A Trick for a Treat
Book Four: Winging It
Book Five: Wrapping Up
Book Six: Loved Up
Book Seven: Rocking Out
Book Eight: Acting Up
Legally Red: A standalone featuring Melissa, with the action occurring between books eight and nine of the main series
Book Nine: Swotting Up
Book Ten: Forget Me Knot
Book Eleven: All Hallowed Out
Holiday Heist: A standalone featuring Melissa, with the action occurring between books eleven and twelve of the main series
Book Twelve: Doing Time (Coming in late 2020)

Wayfair Witches Side Stories:
(These books can be read as standalones, but if you'd like to read them in order with the main series, see the list above for their placement in the series timeline)
Legally Red
Holiday Heist

Books in the Riddler's Edge Series:
Book One: A Little Bit Witchy
Book Two: Witchy See, Witchy Do
Book Three: Lucky Witches
Book Four: Shiver Me Witches
Book Five: So Very Unfae
Book Six: Old-School Witch
Book Seven: A Little Bit Vampy
Slippery Slope: A standalone featuring Pru, with the action occurring between books seven and eight of the main series
Book Eight: A Little Bit Chilly
Book Nine: A Little Bit Spacey
Riddler's Edge Standalones:
Slippery Slope: A standalone featuring Pru, which can be read on its own – if you'd like to read in order with the main series, the action occurs between books seven and eight

Books in the Katy Kramer Series:
Book One: The Case of the Wayward Witch
Book Two: The Case of the Haunted House
Book Three: The Case of the Listening Library
Book Four: The Case of the Strange Society

Boxed Sets:
Riddler's Edge Books 1-3
Wayfair Witches Books 1-3

Made in the USA
Monee, IL
15 January 2021